Soul Survivor

Susan Faw

Cover Design by Greg Simanson
Edited by Pam Harris

This is a work of fiction. Names, characters, places, brands, media, and incidents are either the product of the author's imagination or are used fictitiously. Any resemblance to similarly named places or to persons living or deceased is unintentional.

PRINT ISBN 978-0-9953438-3-2
EPUB ISBN 978-0-9953438-2-5

"Artio, the moon godling, slumped to the horizon, blood red. Helga found her oozing a bloody light across the heavens.
Convinced that her sister was dying, Helga carried her into the bowels of the earth.
The darkness stilled Artio's light.
Helga believed Artio would be reborn as the rest of the mortals of the earth were, but the godling had no one to care for her rebirth and was forever lost.
Caerwyn and Alfreda banished Helga to the depths of the underworld, never to return, for the crime of slaying a godling.

So began the Battle of Daimon Ford."

Excerpt from the Tome of Salvation, Sixth Scribed Copy, Royal Library of Cathair

Chapter 1

Caerwyn

CAERWYN STRODE THROUGH the palatial gardens of Cathair, a royal purple, autumn oak leaf embroidered cape billowing over his rune-enhanced armour plate. The segmented chest sections clicked in time to his hurried stride while his manservant sidestepped and hopped striving to keep up.

The manservant tugged at the flapping leather straps of Caerwyn's metal-studded leather greaves, struggling to tighten them onto his swinging arm, all the while casting anxious glances at his footing. He juggled the king's helmet in the crook of his right elbow and his sword belt over the left.

"One moment, my king!" he puffed. "If you will pause for just a moment, I can complete your battle armour."

Caerwyn growled in response and did not pause until he reached the cool shade created by the towering outer curtain wall. Stone steps led to the battlements at the end of the curving stone walkway that hugged the curtain. Horns blared overhead, long and low, warning of the approach of an enemy force.

"Be about it quickly, Hud." Caerwyn held his arms out at his side, his impatience evident in the tightening of his jaw. Hud swiftly fastened the greaves and swung the sheath of Caerwyn's sword around his waist, buckling it into place before he bowed over the king's helm, an intricately carved metal bowl with large wings decorating both sides and a long nose plate, dividing his face in half.

Caerwyn bent his neck, and Hud slid it onto his head.

Straightening, Caerwyn met Hud's eyes creased with worry. He placed his hand on Hud's shoulder and squeezed gently. "Let us pray it is good news approaching our gates this day for the tidings have been ill as of late." Caerwyn turned and strode away to the stairs, taking them two at a time, his guard of hand-picked Kingsmen hurrying to keep up in his wake.

Hud, pensive and preoccupied, watched the god-king mount the stairs until he vanished from view. With a sigh, he hobbled back in the direction of the armoury. He massaged his hip as he limped across the stony clearing, attempting to ease the annoyingly painful twinges.

Battle is for the young, thought the salt and pepper-haired Hud, but it was an empty thought. He longed for nothing more than to be able to raise his sword in battle once again to defend his king and god.

Hud's sword arm was strong and true, but he could no longer sit a saddle or ride a Pegasus, a requirement of active service in the Kingsmen. Now in retirement, Hud tended the king directly, for even though he could not fly, his skill with a sword and his knowledge of battle had not dimmed. In addition to his duties to his sire, he put whetstone to blade in the armoury and oversaw the care of the winged mounts of the royal stables.

He grabbed the large circular pull on the heavy oak armoury door and pulled, his hip squealing in protest, a personal echo of the rusted hinges. He gritted his teeth then hobbled into the dim interior as the door swung and creaked behind him.

Rows and rows of swords hanging by their hilts on wooden racks met his eyes, glinting in the light streaming from high narrow windows set into the drystone walls. The smell of oil and polishing paste blended with the scent of cedar. He inhaled deeply, and limping over the workbench in the corner, eased himself onto it then took up where he had left off, polishing the flat of a fine curved blade. At least this much of his day was the same. He set to work, and the repetitive action relaxed him and the pain in his hip eased.

He placed the finished sword on the rack beside him then bent to pick up his third sword, laying it on the table and dipped the cloth into the pot of hot oil, when the castle warning bells rang out in alarm.

* * *

Caerwyn cleared the lip of the staircase, pulling his sword as he ran to the battlement to peer down at the approaching army.

A billowing cloud of dust created by the feet of many mounts partially obscured their numbers but was easily spotted by the watchtowers, and the battlement was consequently crowded four deep with fully armed Kingsmen, who parted their ranks for the king as he made his way to his Captain General.

Captain Brennan focused his one good eye on the king, shouldering his way to the front lines, frowning at the king as he strode up to Brennan. Despite his armour-clad form, the king screamed royalty, his purple cape fastened at the throat by an eagle pin.

"Might as well pin a flaming bullseye on your chest," Captain Brennan grumbled audibly. "Who told you weak-willed curs to stand aside?" he bellowed "It's just the flaming king! Back to your positions!" he roared, his drooping mustache quivering.

Caerwyn chuckled as the men attempted to regain their positions without actually touching his royal person. He was by far the tallest man in the contingent and easily peered over their helms as they shifted in front of him.

"Report, Brennan."

Brennan passed the spyglass to Caerwyn, and he placed the narrow tube against his eye. The dust cloud resolved into a multitude of large hairy brown beasts with great curving tusks and legs as large as tree trunks. They were fully plated in armour, including the weak spot located between the eyes. One strike by something as small as a stone would kill them instantly, so they were armoured at all times.

On the back of each beast was a saddle carrying three to four people. They were still a fair distance away, and Caerwyn was unable to determine if the riders were male or female.

"A Primordial host, my lord. They come with their battering mammoths. And there," he pointed off to the left, "are the sabretooths." Caerwyn leaned forward to catch a glimpse of the great cats as they padded around a small hill.

"Have you located Alfreda yet? She must be with the most forward guard."

"Not yet, my lord."

"Well then, I am going out to greet them." Caerwyn turned to head back down the staircase when the warning bells of the watchtowers began to peal.

Surprised, he turned back, just as a large boulder soared over the wall, crashing into the wall of the upper story and knocking a hole straight through the stonework. Crumbling masonry rained down on the Kingsmen and cries rang out, some in pain, some in warning. Caerwyn found himself instantly crushed to the stone surface as the Kingsmen around him threw their bodies at him to physically shield him from the attack.

"Find out where that attack came from!" bellowed Brennan, just as a second boulder soared over the wall, this time striking the base of one of the watchtowers. The impact sent a shudder through the walkway, and then the tower crumbled with a trickle of mortar, quickly joined by a cascade of stone. The tower trembled and with a sharp crack, it toppled, crushing the Kingsmen scrambling to clear the area in time.

Down below, similar projectiles were falling amongst the Primordial ranks, crushing man and beast alike.

Brennan jerked himself upright as he spied more massive stones tumbling from the sky.

"Get the king below. *Now!*"

Brennan hauled the men off of Caerwyn then dragged the king upright by an arm and onto his feet. Caerwyn, spying the confusion and panic of the Primordial forces now trapped outside the castle walls shrugged off the hands of the Kingsmen and grabbed Brennan by his sleeve. "Get the Primordial inside the walls. *Now!*"

Brennan turned and bellowed an order to be carried to the gates. "Open the gates! Open the gates! Sound the horns for sanctuary! Hurry!"

The runners set off, calling out as they ran. The horns on the walls sounded three short blasts followed by a long wail, the universal sounding of sanctuary. The gates shivered then parted, sliding slowly over the gravelly surface. The Primordials on the plain, hearing the call, galloped their mounts toward the safety of the castle walls while the deadly missiles continued to fall all around them.

The gates clanked and ground their way wide open as the Primordial warriors swept across the threshold, following the great cats, who slunk close to the ground, yellow eyes angry, yowling and spitting their displeasure, while the lumbering mammoths bellowed angrily, snorting fire at any that came too close. They swung their great horned heads, creating islands of calm around then while the ground buzzed with warriors.

Caerwyn reached the commons just as the last of the Primordial crossed into the crowded green. His eyes frantically scanned the convulsing crowd, seeking the face of his sister, Alfreda.

Caerwyn pushed his way into the milling mass, giving his guard apoplectic fits as they tried to shield him from all angles in the midst of the panicked crowd. He dodged the gouts of fire that blasted across his path, causing the Kingsman on his right to swear, frantically patting down the flames ignited on his tunic. It was then that he spied her.

She stood unperturbed beside a sabretooth, stroking the cat's sleek head and murmuring to it, her eyes also scanning the milieu. As her beautiful head turned, the sun turned her normally black hair to purple. It curled to her shoulders and one side was tucked behind her tiny ear. Their eyes met across the crowd, and they crinkled into a smile of greeting. Caerwyn rushed over and swung his twin into his arms, whirled her around, and hugged her tight to his chest.

Alfreda hugged him back and as her feet touched the ground once more, her smile faded.

"We must talk," she murmured "Right now and in private."

"Agreed." The bombardment had ceased as soon as the Primordial people reached the sanctuary of the castle. Caerwyn snapped his fingers and a Kingsman stepped forward, saluting. "Find Hud, and bring him to the library." He made to turn away but Caerwyn's hand on his arm halted him. "And I want to know the count of the injured."

"Yes, sir!" He snapped another sharp salute then set off at a jog for the armory.

"This way." Caerwyn took his sister by the elbow, turning her in the proper direction.

"I remember the way, Caerwyn," she said with a tilt of her chin and plunged into the throng.

Chapter 2

Alfreda

ALFREDA WAS SHORT IN STATURE, which was not to say she was diminished. What she lacked in height, she made up for in bearing. She rose only to the tip of Caerwyn's shoulder, yet she parted the crowd by sheer presence. Her people calmed as she passed and bowed low, hands over hearts, a queen amongst her subjects.

Caerwyn bobbled along in his sister's wake, appearing to be little more than her manservant rather than her brother. The only thing destroying this image was his royal armour, but to the Primordial people, it had no more value than the true servant who fell in behind them silently carrying her bags. Alfreda was the mother goddess and the sum total of all things regal and worthy of worship, in the eyes of a Primordial. No other being could come close.

Once clear of the press of people and animals, Caerwyn moved up alongside her and steered her not toward the residences, but toward a round building visible only by the conical shape of the metal-plated roof set back behind a private wall of the garden reserved for royals. Caerwyn produced a large key and let them in through a small garden door set into the limestone wall.

Alfreda's guard and Caerwyn's guard jointly crowded their way through the garden gate and Caerwyn glared at them, frustrated by all the fussing. The kingsmen pointedly avoided meeting his eyes.

He retraced the route he had taken earlier that day, their guards bobbing in their wake like a raft of ducklings. Reaching the library door, Caerwyn halted them with a raised hand. "No one is to enter except Hud, on our command." The dual contingent of guards strung themselves out around the building, reminiscent of a string of festival lanterns but without the gaiety. Caerwyn mounted the steps, Alfreda matching him stride for stride then he slammed the door shut behind them, shutting them away from the crowd.

"You should not treat them so," said Alfreda, her eyes twinkling. "They are protecting you the only way they know how."

"I would have no quibble over it except that I do not need protection. And neither do you."

"From mortal men, yes. But from the gods? That might be different."

"And what, pray tell, are they going to be able to do to shield me from a god's wrath?"

"A distraction perhaps or a lie? They are quite adept at it when they choose to be." Alfreda wandered over to her favourite chair under the tall stained glass windows and curled into the high-backed, overstuffed seat. She tucked her feet under her, disappearing into the tapestry folds of the chair. "I hate to think that our people would betray us, but events are outpacing our knowledge of them. I fear the people no longer pray to the gods." She lifted the lid of the tea pot sitting by her elbow and seeing that it was empty, commanded *"Tea!"* It filled with a hiss and an aromatic citrusy scent filled the air, steam rising from its spout. She tipped the hot brew into her cup, then reached over and filled one for Caerwyn.

Caerwyn's forehead creased into a frown as he sat down heavily, legs splayed, elbows resting on knees. With a deep sigh, he reached over and picked up the waiting cup.

"How many were hurt or killed today? The Kingsmen run around trying to protect me when it should be the other way around. I should be protecting them." He took a sip then put the cup back down with a rattle and grunted. "We are their caretakers, not the other way around. I hate seeing lives wasted, prematurely ended for no good reason. Those deaths out there today should not have happened. Their souls are now our responsibility. It is our fault."

"It is not our fault, and you know it. What *is our problem* and potentially our fault is the escalating problem with Helga. That is why I came to see you," said Alfreda.

"You are closer to her than I am. What is she experimenting with?" Caerwyn asked. "Is she responsible for this? Is it something she and Artio are doing together? I asked Helga outright, and she laughed at me and told me to mind my own business."

Alfreda set her cup down, picked up the pot of tea, and refilled it to the brim.

"Artio is up to something. As the caretaker of the heavens, she is responsible for safeguarding the movements of the stars and planets. It is her domain and her charge. But lately I have noticed that the timing of the planetary movements is off. It is the tiniest of increments, true, but there should be no variation at all. It's almost as though she is absent," she said thoughtfully, shaking her head. "Maybe she is taking a vacation? Absurd as it sounds, she has not been seen for months."

"Well she does like to work undisturbed" said Caerwyn "If something was really wrong, and she was really missing, it wouldn't be a slight problem. It would be catastrophic."

Alfreyda nodded, lips pressed together in puzzlement. "I first noticed it one night when the stars dimmed, as though a haze covered the sky, the moon's timing slightly off. I might not have noticed at all if were not for the butterflies. They are sensitive to the slightest change in the world and are the first to suffer when their environment changes. She frowned. "I think the moon's slippage is creating a disturbance in their internal equilibrium."

Caerwyn grimaced and took another sip of tea, as though to wash away a sour taste. "It's another sign. Artio plays with the planets like she is plucking toadstools in the forest. While they are hers to command, she forgets that she can cause harm to the mortals around her, both animal and human. If she causes their deaths, and then their souls become *our responsibility*. I've begun to notice an influx of human souls beyond the normal. I can only imagine what Helga is doing, shut away in her home under the mountain. Do they not understand that their interference with the natural world is causing calamitous results? People are dying!"

"I know. It's not just people." Alfreda plucked a loose thread in the tapestry of the chair. "I came across a meadow as we travelled this way" she said softly. "It was littered with thousands and thousands of dead butterflies; so many that they carpeted the grass. I wept at the sight. So many fey lives *lost*. Crushed out of existence!" Tears welled and one escaped, sliding down her cheek. "I was not in time to save them."

Caerwyn stood and strode around the room, boots clicking on the tiled floor, restless with the need to act. At that moment, the door opened and Caerwyn paused, turning to see who had entered. Hud limped inside, hugging an object wrapped in cloth to his chest.

"My lady, sire." He bowed at the waist and then approached them, pausing beside the table.

"Hud. Thank you for coming so quickly."

"Of course, sire. How may I assist you?"

"I need your help. Do you remember the patrol three months ago to the base of the Highland Spine at the ford of the river Erinn?"

"How could I forget, sire?" Hud resisted the urge to massage his bad leg, twinging sympathetically at the memory. "It ended my career as a Kingsman."

Caerwyn frowned at the shared memory. "This time, we must penetrate the spells cast around that mountain. Something stirs in its black depths. We must know what it is, if mortal existence is to be preserved."

Hud's grim smile met Alfreda's clear gaze. He bowed deeply to her. "My lady, you will be our guide?"

Alfreda nodded her head in acceptance and turned back to her brother. "I will assist in your search and offer what protection I can. The creatures of the mountain's slopes are yours to command if they may be of assistance," she replied.

"Then may I suggest you make use of this?" Hud placed the wrapped bundle on the table. Caerwyn watched while Alfreda bent over and unwound the parcel.

As the wrappings fell away, a box was revealed. Midnight blue, it was so dark that it absorbed all light surrounding it, making it difficult to define the edges. Magic leaked from the box, peeking out the sides of the lid as though it strove to push back the cover and expand the darkness held at bay. It gave off a faint hum that set Caerwyn's teeth on edge.

"A balance box! Where ever did you find it?" asked Alfreda. "Our father used to speak of them. I thought they were all destroyed."

"This box has been in my family for generations," said Hud. "It has been passed down from father to son for as long as anyone can remember. And now it is my son, Mordecai's. He is the keeper of the box. He has the magic to control it."

Caerwyn backed away from the humming box, unnerved by the power emanating from it. "Why have we not heard of this before?" he asked harshly, his tone sharper than he had intended. "Bring your son to us that we may speak to him of it."

"Of course, sire. I will be but a moment." He bowed, then turned and limped back to the carved door, disappearing through it. It closed with a thud behind him.

"I do not like that box," said Caerwyn. "It is a god-killer." The box shuddered and rattled. It whispered to him, so low that he could not catch its words, but the words shivered and stroked at his soul.

Alfreda ran her hands briskly over her arms in an attempt to smooth the goosebumps pebbling her skin. "Nor do I, but if what stirs in the mountain is what we fear, this may be the only hope we have. We will keep it safe and secure with Hud's son. He must be a wizard if he is able to handle the box. He will be able to control its powers. It is but one challenge we face."

Alfreda stood up and took over Caerwyn's pacing, while he sank into the chair opposite the box and stared at it, refusing to take his eyes from it as though it were a wild beast about to spring.

"The truth is, I believe Artio and Helga are behind the disruptions in the natural world we see around us," said Alfreda. "It might not be intentional, but the effect is the same. The last time I spoke to Artio, she was running off to experiment with the moon, chasing a wild theory of her own making." She paused by the window, eyes caught on the nearly full moon that shone palely in the noon sky. "She believed that slowing its progress would give longer growing days as it exerts gravity on the earth. And Helga, well she never looks much beyond the rock beneath her feet, preoccupied as she is with her tending to the condemned. She never considers the living world. What could possibly bring them together I cannot imagine...if they are indeed working together. We don't actually know that is the case."

Caerwyn stood up and walked over to Alfreda, gripping her shoulder with his left hand and squeezing it in comfort. "We will figure this out before it's too late, you and I together."

They both turned to the sound of the door reopening. Hud limped back into view and at first it appeared he had come alone. Then he shifted slightly. A young child trailed in his wake, brown hair falling in curls to his shoulders around a cherubic face. "This is my son, Mordecai."

The child appeared to be no more than seven summers in age. A big smile wreathed his face at the sight of the king. He ran over and climbed up into the chair beside Alfreda. "I'm hungry!" He settled into the oversized chair then grinned over at a bemused Caerwyn. "Can we have lunch, now, sire?"

Chapter 3

Helga

HELGA STRODE ALONG THE NARROW PATH that ran along the sheer cliff face with an ease of long practice. The midday sun shone directly down, and she pulled the hood of her cloak forward on her head to cut the glare.

She hated the sun. It blinded her to all that moved and made the shadowy reaches of her sanctuary retreat beneath the blazing onslaught. *If I had my way, I would never leave my home.* But Artio had begged her to come see her latest experiment with the moon. *Acch! Who cares about planetary bodies? Cold and remote and eternally boring, like the gods who formed them. For that matter, what good was their useless father, outcast of the gods?* She had long since stopped praying to them.

And then there were the useless twins, the honoured siblings. Favoured by their outcast father and useless mother and pampered by the gods, they were the "golden children" who could do no wrong, at least in their father's eyes. Even in banishment, Morpheus had seen fit to give them the prime real estate on the earth. They were given dominion over the living. But she? She was stuck with the dead, those unredeemable souls, the castaways. She was also cast out for the smallest of crimes. What was the loss when the transformed soul had been banished in the first place? When thousands had been dumped at her rocky doorstep to rot?

She was ashamed of their father, if truth be known. *How could a god lower himself to rut with a mortal woman? Was he insane? I would have banished him too.* She skirted a large bolder and then swerved off to a descending path that led into the shade of some scrubby pines with half their branches missing. Thinking of their father wound her up, her anger bubbling to the surface of her skin and blistering the stone she trod on, leaving a blackened outline of her boot where she stepped.

Flame leapt to her fingertips and the trailing grasses ignited with the heat of her anger. The smell of fresh burn made her withdraw from her introspection and she tamped down her hatred, realizing she was leaving a literal blazing trail of her passing.

Helga glanced at the blue sky overhead, peaking through the tree tops. She could just make out the pale shadow of the moon in the sky. Somewhere beyond it, in the celestial realm, was the home of the gods. Their home wandered across the sky, the nightly reminder of their presence now obscured by the brightness of daylight. *The home of the gods.* Helga snorted. *The gods never visit. They ignore us, their half-mortal half-immortal children, preferring to keep themselves pure and untouched by the bastard offspring of one of their own.* Helga tossed a wet blanket over her thoughts, her temperature rising once again.

Now is not the time to dwell on family history, she thought. *But there will come a time. Oh yes.*

She left the scrubby pines behind her and followed the winding path to where it parted the stunted brush, barren of green growth in the early spring cold that still clung to this side of her mountain home. The bushes ended, and she paused out of long habit to take in her surroundings.

The glen was a flattish field, flush with new shoots of growth, the fuzzy sprouts the first signs of the emerging spring. It was nondescript yet stirred like a kicked anthill. At regular intervals, deep holes sank into the ground beside mounds of freshly turned earth and beside each of these breeches lay grey stones of mammoth size. Helga spotted large groups of men, hauling wooden sleds on runners that slowly inched the stones toward the lip of the pits.

A man stood in the center of the activity, directing the stone's placement. The man was as close to a god as humanity could produce. He stood in the exact center of the maelstrom, a calm epicentre in the yelling, grunting, sweating ring of humanity struggling to tip the stones into their final resting places.

Helga studied him. Even though it was early morning and the dew was not yet gone, he had discarded his overcoat and wore a sleeveless linen shirt tied loosely at the front. Dark chest hair curled through the drawstrings, and his heavy shoulders bulged as he lifted a corded arm to illustrate a shouted instruction. His chin was square and shadowed by a trimmed beard that travelled down his throat. His nose was sharp as an eagle's beak, but it only added to his stature, accenting piercing chestnut eyes, framed by jet black lashes and hair that curled thickly to the nape of his neck.

Genii spotted her standing at the mouth of the glade and waved, motioning to her to come down, flashing a huge smile full of white teeth in her direction. Helga mouth twitched into a semblance of a smile in acknowledgement.

Artio, who she had not noticed until now, rose from the side of one of the stones where she had been instructing the worker on an adjustment to the slip of the sled, brushing dirt from her knees and hands. She wore her favorite sleeveless leather vest and pleated skirt studded with tiger eye cabochon over a chestnut tunic. Her matching lace up boots ran to mid-thigh and fit like a second skin. Tawny brown and sun streaked, her hair tumbled to her mid-back and a long fringe fell over her green eyes. She shoved it back out of her youthful face as she stood up, checking the progress of the other stones. She was the epitome of a young godling, strong and proud and free. She turned toward Genii. Seeing his gaze focused on a point at the entrance to the bowl, she turned and spotted Helga. Artio's smile was as broad as Genii's. With brisk strides, she climbed the short hill to meet Helga.

"What do you think?" Artio yelled over the din of the hammers and the grunts of men, bodies straining to move the fingers of stone.

Helga's eyes strayed back to Genii. *Marvelous form. Quite delicious, really.*

"What is all this?" Helga flicked a hand in the general direction of the glade. "Another temple to the gods?" Derision seeped through in her tone.

Artio did not seem to hear it, for she gushed on, "It's a focus, a radiant focus. It will harness the moon's rays and harvest the latent energy, allowing for the moon's rays to be transformed into a pulled power stream that..."

Helga's eyes glazed over as her mind drifted away from Artio's explanation and back onto Genii. He had left the epicenter, and his long muscular legs carried him over to a slip that was caught up on a rock impeding its forward motion. The runner had dug deep into the soft soil and churned up a large rock just beneath the surface, which was now jammed up against another stone.

He is the epitome of the poetry of the gods. I really must have him for myself.

Genii bent down and, with the strength of three men and the assistance of two, lifted the skid over the offending stone and placed it back down on the clear path where it shot forward by several inches as it was suddenly freed.

Genii walked to the other side of the stone across the landing pit and pulled an instrument from his pocket, checking the alignment of the rock. When he was satisfied, he checked the other eight's bearings. He went from group to group and stopped their work as the stones' alignment was verified. The seventy-odd men who'd toiled the morning to pull the stones into place put down their ropes and slumped wearily, grateful for the rest.

Artio, noticing Helga's glassy-eyed vacant stare, turned back to the valley and with exclamation of "Oh, never mind!" ran back down to Genii.

Genii watched her come, an even wider smile on his patrician face, eyes crinkled with caring. Artio skidded to a halt in front of him and grabbed his muscular arm to stop her slide, and Genii's hand grasped her waist to stop her motion. He held her for a moment and his gaze was so tender, *so smitten*, it was impossible to miss.

Jealousy and a pure white rage spiked within Helga's chest. She carefully masked the emotions and, pasting a smile on her face, regally descended into the glade.

She approached the couple and they broke apart, oblivious to her jealousy. "It's time to set the stones. Come look!" Artio grabbed Helga's hand and tugged her over to examine a large stone lying on its side. At least twenty feet tall, the massive stone was freshly chiseled with likenesses of the gods, the elements, and the living creatures inhabiting the earth.

Artio chatted away about the various methods the stones would harvest and channel the moon's energies. "See this picture?" She placed a hand on a carving of a bear. "This image rune can bring forth the spirit bear! The spirit bear is my favourite! I wish I could be a spirit bear. They are so regal and intelligent. Did you know…?" Helga's eyes glazed over once again, distracted by the form of Genii who had unfurled a parchment and was now consulting the schematic, his arms holding the papyrus at an angle to compare the drawings against the current configuration of stones.

"…and when all the stones are perfectly aligned, they will be able to heal anything within the circle. It's a medicine wheel, see? But this one is powered by the celestial bodies, the moon specifically. Did you hear me, Helga?"

Helga started and then turned back to Artio. "Yes, medicine wheel. Very nice," she said in a bored voice that dripped sarcasm. She spun around and walked back to the path.

"Where are you going?" shouted Artio.

"I have matters to attend to," said Helga with a lazy wave over her shoulder. "I do not want to keep you from your building."

"But I want you to see how it works!" yelled Artio.

"Call me when you have it working, and I will come back for a demonstration." The words drifted back into the vale as Helga disappeared into the brambles. As she entered the overhang of the scraggly pines, a thought surfaced. *The only way I will return to this vale, is if there is something in it for me...or someone. What a bloody waste of time.*

Chapter 4

Artio

THEY LABOURED LONG INTO the afternoon after an hour's rest to eat and drink. As the final stones slipped into their berths, the evening's western rays settled on the clearing. The remaining workers raked the last of the freshly churned soil around the base of the freestanding stones, tamping it into place.

Artio peered at the angle of the sun and smiled. So many times, she had come to this spot with Papa because of the magical way the sun's rays lanced through the valley between the mountain peaks. The precision of it thrilled her, and her medicine wheel playset had performed every bit as well as the real thing.

Artio smiled, remembering the tiny dead sparrow she'd placed at the convergence of the rays, its neck broken. The setting sun triggered the runes on the tiny stones. A liquid flame shot around the circle of little pillars and then converged on the stiff bird. A small tremor quivered under her feet and two stones toppled, but when the flash of light faded and the blinking spots in her vision passed, there sat the sparrow, wings quivering. Then with a squawk, it flashed up into the trees.

It was then that Artio knew that she would return and build the medicine wheel but on a much grander scale with full granite monoliths that would withstand the test of time. To be able to bring such a gift to humanity made her heart sing with joy. A tiny frown creased her brow. Helga just didn't understand. Artio believed that life should be lived to the fullest, and one should die with the fullness of days, not in an accident or due to sickness or ill health.

She shoved the thought aside and ran over to Genii, slipping her hand into his. His eyes crinkled into a smile in return, his smile a wordless caress to match the feeling of warmth at her touch. He drew her to the side to watch the workers sprawled in the center of the ring. Exhausted from the day's toil and with various aches and pains from the journey called life, they stood amidst the circle of their own free will, wanting to test the effect of what their labour had wrought.

The sun settled into its final resting place until its rebirth in the eastern morning sky. The rays touched the guardians perched at the top of the wheel of stone and the deeply carved images glowed, first with the light striking their exterior but then the surface flush faded and an inner light flared in the eyes of the guardians. The columns shuddered and a wave of light spread down lighting the runes internally then flashed around the circle. The ground shook with mighty tremors yet nothing toppled. Outside the circle, nothing stirred.

With the last gasp of light from the setting sun, the healing light of the medicine wheel whitened and disappeared. Blinking back the light streaks in her eyes, Artio could see the workers peering hesitantly around at each other and then running hands over their bodies, examining hands and old scars and missing appendages which had suddenly reformed. Cries of shock and joy erupted from the circle, but those were not what attracted Artio's eyes.

The ghostly forms of animals rose from the meadow, restored to their spirit form from deaths that should not have been. Artio was sure the others could not see them, but they were there nonetheless. She frowned. *Someone has been hunting and slaying the animals of the Primordial forests but to what purpose? What could be important enough to deny them their rebirth? I will speak to Alfreda about this. This is her area of expertise.*

"Wonderful!" Artio clapped her hands together, celebrating the healing of the workers, who surged forward to show her that their fingers had regrown straight and youthful, that their scars had vanished, and eyesight had strengthened. "Go share your joy with your families. Remember that the medicine wheel will only work during this moon cycle each year with the alignment of the spring solstice. Remember the gods and honour their spirits for giving you this great gift!"

The workers bowed and scraped and then vanished out of the glade, eager to return to their kin to share the joyous news.

Artio turned back to the circle of rock eyes running over their towering forms. They were quiet and still, as they had been when erected "Now the real work begins, Genii. Help me fine tune the alignment. We have a week before the full moon arrives. We must be ready by then, if we hope to capture this phase of it." She gathered his hands in hers, running her thumbs over his calloused palms, and then peered up into the warm depths of his eyes. "Then and only then can we truly be one for all eternity."

Genii kissed her, a gentle kiss full of shared hope and longing, mixed with awe and trepidation. Although Artio acted as any normal human female, she was not a human, or at least fully human. That fact alone would have terrified any normal mortal, but Genii wasn't a normal human male. He was a bastard who happened to be a wizard.

Chapter 5

Caerwyn

MORDECAI SAT MUNCHING on a ham and cheese sandwich from a rapidly emptying tray brought in by a servant. He alternated bites between a tottering stack of sandwiches and an equally large pile of crunchy pickles, fresh from the pickle vat of the kitchens. Caerwyn pulled Hud to the side of the room by his shirt sleeve while Alfreda distracted the child with tales of the woods that were her home when she lived amongst the Primordials. Occasionally, she snuck a pickle from Mordecai's stack. Mordecai's eyes followed the stolen pickle, as though missing one would cause him to go hungry.

Across the room, an argument in hushed tones was being carried out.

"...You suggest that we give control of this box *to a child?* Hud, even a full grown wizard would struggle to control the danger of this box," muttered Caerwyn. "It contains a great evil. If it were to be activated or even worse seized by the wrong company, they could destroy the world. There is no room for failure in this. He is too young!"

"Sire, you speak as if magic is something that is learned. I assure you, it is not. You are either gifted with it by the gods or you are not. Did you have to learn to be a godling? No. You simply *are* a godling. It is a part of your very being, the fabric of your existence. He is the same. Mordecai could do things before he could speak. He does not need to be taught how to control the box. He is controlling it right now."

Caerwyn looked over at the box and the boy, alarmed, and Hud grinned. "It has been part of him since birth. No one understands its working better than Mordecai. If there is a great evil to be fought, he is the boy for the job."

"He is but a child!" Caerwyn protested. "He cannot go to battle!"

His father shook his head. "He may be a child in years, but there is an old man tucked away inside, at times I see it in his eyes, a wisdom and experience far beyond his years. I believe he was put here to help you." Hud's eyes glazed over as he thought about his words.

Caerwyn sighed and turned back to Alfreda, who was now laughing at something the child had said, her eyes sparkling. Mordecai met Caerwyn's eyes and his eyes beckoned to Caerwyn in invitation. He slowly walked back to the table, studying the child as he drew closer then knelt down next to Mordecai's chair, bringing his eyes on level with the boy. Mordecai's sparkling blue eyes twinkled, and he placed his hand on Caerwyn's shoulder.

"Do not be afraid, sire. I understand the box. I know how it works. I can help you." Mordecai picked up the box and wrapped it back up in the soft cloth hiding it from view. It did not seem to affect him as it did them. Mordecai looked up and smiled at the bemusement in their gazes as he handled the box without harm.

Caerwyn smiled back at him and patted his knee. "Thank you, Mordecai, I accept your offer of assistance. Mind if I steal one of those sandwiches?"

Chapter 6

Alfreda

THE CASUALTIES FROM THE BOMBARDMENT were not as severe as originally thought. Two dead, their souls passing into Caerwyn's care, and fifteen injured and now being treated in the hospital wing of the castle.

Alfreda visited each Kingsmen or Primordial in the infirmary, murmuring a kind word of thanks for their service.

On exiting the infirmary, she joined Caerwyn and they climbed to the outer wall to examine the massive stone still sitting on the wall where it had landed. They were surrounded by guards, which made the upper wall extremely crowded and, to Caerwyn's mind, advertised their presence to the enemy if indeed the attack had been targeted.

The massive stone was as polar opposite to the limestone blocks forming the castle walls as it was possible to be. It was roughly a comet in shape, as though it had been formed by the wind passing over it. The surface was greyed and bubbled. Small fissures and craters pockmarked the surface. Alfreda bent down and picked up a chunk of stone that had fractured off the main rock with the impact. Inside, a smooth, tar-coloured glass was revealed. She turned it over in her hands, frowning.

She turned back to Caerwyn and handed him the chunk. "This is the evidence we needed. Look at the composition of this rock. This is obsidian, part of a lava flow. This was not an attack but an eruption."

She walked over to the wall and gazed down at the approach. Great stones dotted the hillside, some large enough to leave large gouges of overturned earth as they skidded and bounced to their final resting places. The sizes ranged from massive rocks like the one beside them to stones no bigger than a human head.

"But the question is what is causing the eruptions? And where are they coming from? What do you think of the angle of the impacts?" She lifted her arm and pointed in a northwesterly direction. "I think they have come from there."

Caerwyn followed the line of sight produced by her outstretched arm. "That would put it in the Highland Needle, near the pass, possibly just above the ford of the River Erinn."

"Yes, that is what I was thinking too, very near to Helga's home at the edge of her domain, her *protected* domain." Alfreda leaned on the wall, studying the patterns. "What could she possibly be up to that would cause breaches in the mountain? Or is this a natural phenomenon of some sort? Do you think Artio is visiting her right now?"

"It's possible."

"Then I will return and see if I can talk to Helga. She is on my doorstep. Perhaps she does not know of the eruption," Alfreda shook her head slowly from side to side, "but I do not see how that is possible. The mountain must rumble with the building pressure. Earthquakes would be a natural side effect of such a breach."

"I do not like the idea of you confronting her alone." Caerwyn took his sister's elbow and steered her toward a door set in the wall that lead to an interior corridor of the castle. The sweep of guards followed. "If you will give me a few days, I will gather my Kingsmen and then we can present a unified front to Helga. The last visit to her realm did not go well and several of my Kingsmen were injured trying to reach Helga to chat. She has put up defences against unwanted visitors and it seems we head that list. It would have been nice if she had warned us and the fact she did not," he grimaced, "means she did not care who came to visit. That, of and by itself, is alarming. She has become reclusive as of late."

"Agreed." Alfreda paused just inside as she crossed the threshold into the castle's interior, allowing her eyes to adjust to the dim interior. "All right, I will stay until you are prepared and we will leave together. We will make her see reason. I would like a word with my clansmen, so that we may prepare a plan of action."

"Your normal suites have been prepared for you and your chiefs. I will leave you to your discussions and we can meet again for dinner in the grand hall."

Alfreda hugged Caerwyn and with a smile, she walked off down the right hallway, gathering her guard as she disappeared down the tiled floor, her steps sure and confident, a queen amongst her people.

Chapter 7

Hud

MORDECAI SKIPPED ALONG beside his father, holding his hand and chatting about how nice the king and the Primordial queen were and that they made about the best sandwiches in the world. Hud carried the blanket-wrapped balance box under his arm and matched his steps to his son's as he retraced the familiar path back to their lodgings, tucked into a corner of the castle wall part way between the door to the kitchens and the large stable that housed the horses.

Reaching the front door, Mordecai waved his hand and the door swung open on silent hinges before he could place a hand on the latch. For Mordecai, the things he could do were as natural as breathing, things that made others stop and stare.

The box had been handed down to his family for safekeeping longer than anyone could remember. Hud had no magical ability, but his mother had been a witch of immeasurable ability. Somehow it had skipped him, though. When she died, he had despaired that the ability had been lost. It was after her death that he and his wife conceived and gave birth to Mordecai, who was now the end of the line.

Hud's wife had died giving Mordecai life, as was often the case where magic was involved. The birth of magic often demanded a life for a life. It was a reason that magic was dying out in the realm, and matches were hard to find, as no one would consciously give their daughter's hand only to find that they died due to the magic coursing through the child's veins. Consequently, the few wizards to exist in the world were often born to whores and lived a rough life on the streets, often falling to a knife or to disease before reaching an age where they could take conscious control of their magic. They were a dying breed on the cusp of extinction.

Mordecai, on the other hand, flourished within the castle walls. Protected physically by their impenetrability, his mind nourished by the best library in the kingdom, he studied the history of the lands and people, both mortal and mythical that abided within it. By the tender age of five, he had mastered the ancient language of the gods and could read the ancient texts without assistance. Now, at the age of seven, he carried the knowledge of a man ten times as his years. What he lacked was experience.

Yet that lack of experience did not hold him back, just as Hud had told Caerwyn. Hud stopped in front of the cabinet built into the wall of the kitchen beside the fireplace and reaching around the side of it, found the hidden latch and pulled. There was a click and he tugged on the front of the cabinet, which swung open on giant hinge, revealing a hidden closet. It was here that the box had been stored for millennia, safe and secure within the stone wall. At the back of the closet was a trap door embedded into the floor that led to a set of tunnels running under the castle.

Hud placed the box on a shelf and then pushed the cabinet door closed. Once it clicked into place, there was no telling that it was anything other than what it appeared to be, a functional kitchen cupboard.

Mordecai was still chattering away but as his father stopped in front of him, he paused long enough to look up at his whiskered face.

"I know. It's time for me to study...uh, father?" Mordecai asked his face hopeful.

"What is it?"

"Can I go with you this time? When the king goes to meet his other sisters?"

Hud studied his son for a moment and then nodded.

"Yippee!" shouted Mordecai, and he clambered onto his chair and pulled the books forward. "This time, I get to see the real thing. This time I get to see the gods up close."

"And why are you so anxious to see them up close?" asked his father.

"Because of this!" Mordecai pulled a skinny book from the pile and shoved it at his father. It was entitled *Prophetic Musings: The War of the Gods*. He did not need to read further to know who had written it. The last witch or wizard with prophetic ability had died years ago. It was written by Hud's mother.

Chapter 8

Artio

THE FOLLOWING MORNING dawned grey and overcast. The rain, hinted at by the pink clouds of the previous evening's setting sun, had settled in, obscuring the top of the ash-filled clouds ringing the peak of the smoking mountain. Fog had sunk onto the clearing floor, so that the monolithic stones appeared to be floating in the sky. Only erected for a day, they nevertheless gave an impression of great age and exuded air of mystery.

Artio witnessed none of these things as she'd left the meadow in the predawn hours, travelling deep into the Primordial forest, Genii at her side. In order for the bonding of the moon to work, there were certain elements that had to be gathered from the misty woods, elements only found there.

The plan had been Genii's from the beginning. Of course, Artio had agreed to the plan as soon as he had proposed it. They were in love, weren't they? The only thing keeping them from being together was his mortality. He had lived longer than most humans due to the magic coursing through his veins, but he would still succumb to old age in time and die, something Artio could not fathom or accept.

So they'd hatched the plan and what could be more eternal than the moon? Tying his life force to the celestial would ensure that his aging was tied directly to the moon's aging and would be so slow as to be unnoticeable. Still not immortal in the true sense, but close enough as to not matter.

Locating the binding agents, now that was the true challenge. For the magic to work, Genii's blood must be bound to the light cast on a full moon, and not just any full moon, but the master moon of the spring equinox. The equinox was the time for rebirth when the sun and moon are equal partners in the sky. The balance of the celestial bodies of moon and world, mimicking the relationship between lovers, would make the magic possible.

Artio pushed through the dense underbrush, the wet leaves slapping against her legs. The object of their search was not far ahead. They had watched the trajectory carefully and had set out as soon as it hit the atmosphere.

The chunk of moon rock came into view, the crush of vegetation an arrow pointing to its final resting place.

"Finally, we have found it! It tumbled further than we figured." Genii took the cape from around his shoulders and gave it a shake to dislodge the moisture dripping from its oiled surface.

"But we have found it, finally," said Artio, quickening her steps. "Please let there be enough," she prayed out loud.

Genii took her hand and knelt on the ground beside a tree trunk with scorch marks on its bark. He parted the ferns and there it was a chunk of moon rock the size of his fist. The colour of ash, it was jagged on all exposures, some protrusions sharp and spiky and some smoothed. To Artio, it looked more like a cockle burr than a rock.

She dropped Genii's hand then pulled out a cloth from her satchel, draping it over the stone. She picked it up and wrapped the cloth securely around the moon rock, careful not to touch it with her bare flesh and then tucked it away deep in her satchel.

Artio stood up, beaming. "We've got it!" She flung her arms around him and kissed him full on the lips, and he snugged her close, kissing her back.

"You are my joy, shade of my heart. Whatever did I do to deserve you for eternity?" he rumbled against her hair. "The day you found me on the streets my life changed. I can never repay you for your love, for your kindness. I love you, Artio, and will love you till the moon crashes into the sea."

"As street urchins go, you were adorable." Drawing back, she swept the fringe of hair off his forehead and smiled, remembering the small boy. "My heart was lost the moment I saw you." She stroked his cheek, eyes alive with the tenderness of love returned. "But the adult man is so much more. You are worthy of a goddess's love."

"You saved me." His eyes darkened slightly with memory. "I would be dead by now, if you had not taken me in."

"Yes, but even then I knew you were special," she said, "that you were unique. We were meant to be together. It is a blessing of the gods."

"And so we shall be together forever." He lowered his forehead to touch hers and kissed the bridge of her nose. "Together...always."

Chapter 9

Caerwyn

THE KINGSMEN BARRACKS were located on the western side of Cathair, outside the castle walls and tucked up tight against the outer ring wall where it joined with the castle itself. A postern gate allowed for the pasturing of the horse herds in a Y formed by the tributary of Cathair Lake to the south and the crumbling ancient stone wall of the old town pastures. They were overgrown with grasses and lichen, the roots sinking deep into the dirt of time's passing. These walls remembered when the god, Morpheus had made Cathair his home, not just his descendants.

Morpheus' creation of humanity was initially considered trivial, a curiosity to the other Gods. Almost on a dare, he formed the people of the world from the native elements: purest air provided by the abundant plant life, virginal waters of mountain streams fed from the snow-capped mountain tops, and the physical essence of the planet – soils so fertile that the planet exploded with life. Morpheus mixed fire and spirit into this raw mould and then breathed the breath of a God into his creation.

The result was miraculous.

He'd created not one, but two unique life forms and then watched as the first people multiplied until they filled every corner of the world. The other Gods applauded his ingenuity, smiling down on the little planet. Amused with the scurrying creatures, they indulged Morpheus, congratulating him on creating a new life form that thrived in the primitive climate. The Gods began to visit the planet and *played* with the people, as though they were pets. They set up palaces in the most beautiful of locations and the world became a vacation paradise for the bored immortals.

Impressed, they asked Morpheus to repeat the process and create life on other worlds. That is, until Morpheus fell in love with one of his creation, a mortal woman, and took her for wife.

When they learned of the union, the Gods were horrified, for they saw the people as little more than animals. Morpheus debased himself in their eyes and in a unanimous decision it was decreed that he must give up his mortal wife.

Morpheus refused. For what he had done, Morpheus was cast down to the earth and his return to the gods barred for as long as he kept his mortal wife. The Gods were forbidden to visit the planet and the planet was decreed off limits for all immortals.

When they abandoned the people of the world, their palaces fell in ruin, but two were preserved; the primordial temple in Faylea and a large castle built on the present day site of Cathair. The others were angrily smashed by the gods, grinding the pieces to dust until only broken jagged pieces of the original foundation stones could be found. Even these had been swallowed by time, and reclaimed by the earth. Never again were the Gods seen in Cathair, nor was it said that the gods protected Cathair. They turned their backs on the people of the world. Out of this rubble, the current castle was built by the people for the heir to Cathair, for the Spirit Shield guardian, the sole son of Morpheus. So it was that the current-day Castle Cathair was formed.

Caerwyn enjoyed walking along the top of the remnant of the ancient walls, for he felt closer to his father during these strolls. He balanced his footing on the slippery moss-covered rocks, hopping from one to the next, while his ever-present guard trailed along behind him, amused at his antics.

He reached a corner of the wall, where a platform stood mostly intact, and climbed up the structure, despite the shouted warnings and appeals for caution. Balancing on the flattish rock, he peered out toward the Spine examining the clouds that gathered around its peak. Despite the watery sun currently washing the field, he could see that real rain was falling at its base.

It would be a journey of three days, maybe four if the weather turned foul, and both man and beast would be slowed by the accompanying slick mud. That many feet and hooves and paws would churn the roads into a malaise of clinging clay that became heavier by the step. The most direct route was a twisting path that swung perilously close to the swamps to the northwest.

Although normally a faster route, the delays along the main road would become substantially longer if their equipment became stuck in the mud slick roads. At least the swamps had solid paths that drained well, but there were other hazards to an army along the edges of the swamps.

In the end, it was decided to divide the armies as this would also allow them to approach the mountain from two directions and hopefully surprise what might be waiting for them when they arrived, if anything stirred in the area.

Caerwyn's horse-backed Kingsmen would take the swamp route and Alfreda would take her people along the Cathair Road with the plan to meet up again at the River Erinn ford where the shallow waters afforded a safe crossing. On the other side, a well-travelled trail led into the high passes, the gateway into the Primordial lands to the north. This plan also had the optical advantage of a people returning home, rather than a people coming to invade, as would be the case if he moved the Kingsmen across too soon.

Caerwyn wondered if Helga would even care to note the difference. She did not own the passes, but as they came very close to her home, both human and Primordial skirted the area, fearful of upsetting a descendent of the gods.

He climbed back down to ground level. As he straightened came eye to eye with his general, Captain Brennan. His one good eye glared at Caerwyn. Even though his lips did not move, he could hear the accusation all the same. He held up his hand to ward off the impending lecture and instead asked "How soon will we be ready to move out?"

"As soon as my liege returns to the castle. Your Pegasus is saddled and awaits you."

"Excellent! What are we waiting for?" Caerwyn strode off across the field and away from his general's angry stare.

He entered through the open gate. As soon as he stepped through, a cacophony of sound assailed his ears. Trumpets blared from the top of the walls at his appearance and the various animals and soldiers stirred with the announcement. Caerwyn spotted Alfreda, already mounted on a sabretooth, leaning forward to scratch the great cat behind its ear.

Caerwyn's favorite Pegasus was an ebony winged creature named Brimstone, fiery-eyed and fierce. Brimstone stamped his hooves impatiently, anxious to be in the air. The rest of the Kingsmen rode ordinary horses, but they were the best breeding stock to be found, deep-chested and long-legged. They could handle any terrain and battle on the flats as well.

With a cheer from the watching crowd, Caerwyn mounted Brimstone and took off into the air soaring in slow circles over Cathair. The main gates swung open and the legion of Kingsmen spilled out into the streets, heading for the open spaces beyond the village of Upper Cathair.

From the sky, Caerwyn could see the entire town below, laid out within the circles of confusion. Semi-concentric ring walls converged on a common focal point within the castle perched on the edge of cliffs falling to the ocean below. A natural barrier, it had yet to be breeched and made an impenetrable defense on the southernmost tip of the peninsula.

The main branch of the combined army snaked through the wall the way they had entered via the broad approach that spilled from the hills on the eastern flank. They skirted the main town and rejoined the central road, a twisting trail clearly visible from the air.

They journeyed together for several hours, the descent a lazy sloping to the great plains.

Brimstone could move faster than the armies, and Caerwyn settled the Pegasus at the agreed location, which was a bend in the river that slowed the waters and afforded a natural watering hole for a large quantity of beasts. Here, he would cross with the Kingsmen. The swamp lay a few miles to the west and already he could feel the muggy air that enveloped the place. It was said to be the birthplace of magic for those few who still possessed the ability.

He was anxious to see what Hud's son made of the place. Many a twisted beast was said to live in the swamps, the imperfect experiments of the gods or the dabbling of wizards and witches gone wrong. None of them were mythical beings like his Pegasus. Everyone knew the mythical were those reborn from a mortal animal's existence.

The mythical creatures were Alfreda's charge, not his. His was the protection of the souls of humanity. That was his to command, his to protect.

But the swamp creatures fell under no one's mandate and were generally left alone, not protected, but not challenged either. Some rudimentary villages had sprung up in the swamp, most of the unsavory kind. They paid neither taxes nor homage but kept to themselves and ignored the world at large.

Caerwyn leaned forward in his saddle, studying the approaching Primordial army, three thousand strong. They crested the hill and spilled over the rise, like so many pebbles sliding down a rock slide.

Chapter 10

Helga

HELGA STROLLED THROUGH the infested village, her nose wrinkling in disgust at the putrid smells of rotting fish and vegetation that clung to simply everything. It did not matter which set of the suspended bridges one chose. They all crossed the same fetid swamp. Swinging rope bridges barely cleared the thick, black waters. A deck of reeds, slick with damp, made the passage treacherous underfoot, even without the swaying movement inherent to its construction. Occasionally, she glimpsed a long snakelike body, rolling just under the surface, smooth and sleek and way too long for her liking.

If she had had her choice, she would not have been there at all. Yet the person she was searching for called the Village of Morass-Fen home, so she traversed the quagmire to a hut perched like a squat tree house at the end of a swing bridge. The leaves of a nearby swamp belly fern shaded it from view, so that the house appeared at first to be only a door with a string of small desiccated skulls hanging on a knotted cord as a door knocker. Helga lifted the skull necklace and let it drop. It made a tinkling sound as the skulls struck the hollow reeds behind them.

The door slowly opened of its own accord in invitation, and Helga ducked through the low entrance, straightening as she cleared the threshold.

A woman sat in a low chair by a flickering fireplace of cedar and stone, the flame warming and providing a low-level lighting to the shadowed interior. Helga was instantly at home in the room, the shadows pleasing to her. She took a step and then halted as she bumped into an invisible barrier.

"Calleigh granted you entry, but she did not invite you to sit." The woman shifted and the firelight bounced off a face full of crags and wrinkles. "Only welcomed guests are to sit."

Helga frowned but quickly smoothed her face and stepped back from the barrier. "Many pardons, madam. I did not mean to barge into your home. I came to the village to seek your assistance."

"Calleigh is not a fairy godmother granting the wishes of strangers or foolish young women...or even foolish young godlings. Calleigh's skills are sought by both the high and the low and by those who seek a magic beyond their own or that they simply cannot perform. Which do you seek today, godling?"

Helga's eyes widened, surprised by her words. She was positive that her disguise was impenetrable. She appeared to be a young woman of perhaps twenty with dark red hair and dressed in the peasant clothing of a local farm wife. The ties of her neckline dangled, and a deep V displayed more cleavage than Helga had intended. The clinging moisture of the swamp beaded on her skin and rolled down the convenient channel on her chest.

"I do not know what you mean, madam," she stuttered, attempting to sound contrite and shy at the same time.

The witch laughed, her eyes reflective as a cat's in the bright firelight. "Calleigh would know Helga even if she dressed like a harlot of the swamp. There is no mistaking a daughter of Morpheus." She looked her up and down. "Even if she *is* dressed like a harlot."

Helga blushed and made to step forward, forgetting the shield, and once again was rebuffed. "Fine, if you insist." The deception dissolved and her normal features returned, and a black dress of fine silk molded to her form. Her rough cloak morphed into a fur-lined cape with a deep hood. "Is this more to your liking, madam?"

"It is a truthful image, even if the reasons for the journey are less than honest." She grabbed the handle of a cane resting against her chair and pulled herself to her feet, hobbling over to the transparent wall that held Helga at the door. As Calleigh wobbled into the firelight, what Helga had thought was a cane was revealed to be the thigh bone of a beast, the upper joint carved into a handle.

"You may enter, but you may not leave until Calleigh grants it. While in my home, you are my guest. The minute you leave, we are once again…less than friends. You may take only what Calleigh gives to you willingly. To take anything not freely given will trigger a curse you will not survive. Do you understand and agree to these terms?"

Helga nodded curtly, curbing her annoyance at the restrictions.

I am no common thief, she thought, *but I am an uncannily good one when I choose to be.* Helga stood regally by the door as the old crone hobbled closer to the doorway and touched a talisman hanging on the pole. The restriction vanished and she turned and hobbled back to her chair, lowering herself painfully into the blanket-covered seat.

"Why does a daughter of Morpheus pay Calleigh a visit?" she asked, settling the blankets back over her knees. She invited Helga to sit with a flick of her hand, directing her to a straight-backed chair set to the right of the fireplace.

"I have need of a potion," Helga said as she settled onto the proffered chair, "and I have heard that you are particularly adept at the blending of potions and elixirs. The potion I seek will bind the will of a foe to me, one born of myth and magic."

Calleigh's watery blue eyes studied the godling but did not ask questions. "Calleigh may have a rendering that would suit your desires but, as with all things, there is a cost. Are you willing to pay this? The price of an enslaving elixir is steep, even for a godling."

Helga's eyes narrowed. "What is this cost?"

"In order for the potion to bind properly, the one who is creating the binding link is also bound in return. It is a symbiotic relationship. The souls of the two individuals are merged at their core. Think of it as Siamese twins, but rather than a physical connection, a shared heart or arm or leg, it is a spiritual one. Sever the bond and you both will die. So Calleigh asks once again. Is this a price that you, godling Helga, are willing to pay?"

Helga stared into the shimmering eyes of the witch, weighing her options. "And what, exactly, is the price *you demand*? You must have a price."

"Calleigh's price is simple. Protect my son Genii. I feel an ill breeze on the air. A foul storm rapidly approaches. I fear for my child, that I will not be able to save him from the approaching calamity, a calamity that is somehow associated with you. A great darkness swirls around him when he visits." She grimaced, as though the taste of the bargain was sour in her mouth. "My price is fair. Do not allow harm to come to him. Swear that you will forfeit your eternity before his. Do this and you shall have the potion you so greatly desire."

Helga was silent while she considered the terms. *Without the elixir, everything I have put into play will fail. I need that elixir before the full moon...but there is more than one way to interpret the deal. They are but words.*

"The deal is struck. I will pay your price, and I swear with my eternal soul that Genii will not die for all eternity. The deal is struck!" she intoned.

"The deal is struck," Calleigh repeated then clapped her wrinkled hands together. A gong sounded sealing the pact. "Let us begin."

A double bind. Genii will be protected for all eternity now. Thank you, daughters of Morpheus.

Calleigh smiled grimly to herself as she prepared the potion.

Chapter 11

Mordecai

MORDECAI BOUNCED ALONG on the seat of the wagon beside his father, as the wheel hit a deep rut along the roadside at the little used fork of the road. He twisted in his seat to watch the Primordial warriors and their fantastic beasts disappear over the crest of the hill behind him then leaned back in his seat as far as he could for as long as he could to keep them in sight. A copse of trees swallowed the view. He gave up and turned back to facing forward.

"I wish I could have a sabretooth," he moaned for the fifth time since leaving Cathair.

Hud grinned at his son. "You can have one when you are grown, if you learn how to take care of one. They are highly intelligent, you know. Do not be fooled into seeing a sabretooth as a pet."

Mordecai frowned at his father and kicked the wooden slat at the front of the wagon with his boot. "I know that, Father. I spoke to Cinda, the one that Alfreda is riding. She is really nice!" he grinned, revealing a missing tooth in his gaping smile. "She let me scratch her behind her ears and everything!"

They bounced along in silence again for a while. Then, with a glance at the creaking leather seat beside him on which sat the cloth bundle containing the box, Mordecai said, "The box is humming."

"Humming? What do you mean, by humming?" This time Hud did look directly at his son.

"It's vibrating and I can hear it." He frowned at the wrapped parcel sitting between them on the seat. "It has a voice, but it is not strong enough for me to understand it yet. But it is getting stronger and louder. Where ever we are going, it likes it."

"That is a lot to gather from a vibrating parcel."

"It's not the box, Papa. It is what's inside the box that is humming."

"Something is inside the box?" Hud asked sharply.

"Oh yes!" said Mordecai happily. "There is something alive inside the box."

Hud's frown deepened. He would bring this up with Caerwyn when they stopped. Perhaps it was not wise to leave his son in sole possession of the box, and perhaps he was the only one it was safe to leave in possession of it. Was the entity in the box evil or benign or neutral? Was it even alive? Mordecai seemed to think so, and he had found his son to be extremely accurate in matters of magic.

"Keep it close to you, Son, but do not open it for any reason. I am serious about this request. Understand?"

"I won't open it. I don't need to. I can talk to it without opening the box."

"It may ask you to, though. Do not do what it asks unless you speak to me or Caerwyn first. This is not a request. It is a command. This is not a game."

Mordecai looked up from where his hand rested on the top of the box, meeting his father's serious eyes and nodded. "I will not open the box unless you say that I can."

Hud reached over and ruffled Mordecai's curls. "You are a good boy."

Mordecai's eyes drifted closed as he tried to sort through the humming to find the words buried in the buzz. It wasn't clear enough yet, but it *was* getting stronger.

They bounced along the dried rutted track for the better part of the day, munching on biscuits, but as they came closer to the village of Morass-Fen the hard ruts softened and smoothed and the humidity rose until Mordecai shed his tan coat. The flies thickened and were joined by bog bugs, which buzzed his ears and tried to land on his exposed skin. His father swatted any that got too close but still by the time the sun sunk toward the horizon, he had several itchy welts to occupy his hands.

As the village jounced into sight, Mordecai's jaw dropped. The entire village *dangled*, impossibly suspended from ropes that disappeared into the canopy overhead. Large mangrove trees with roots running in every direction dotted the dark waters as if they were out for a stroll on a spring evening. The source of the swarms of pests was revealed to be a burping swamp, the surface of which was rarely still. Creatures large and small snapped at the feast of flying annoyances that flitted over the bubbling surface. The coats abandoned earlier were dragged back over bare flesh in an attempt to ward off the bloodsucking insects.

The main body of Kingsmen hung back from the village as all approaches had to be on foot. Caerwyn, Mordecai, Hud, and several Kingsmen guards continued on and stepped onto the boardwalk, which swayed and creaked as their weight settled on the first of the bridges. Hollowed gourds chuckled as they walked, announcing their presence to any who listened.

Mordecai's head swiveled side to side taking everything in. He slipped his hand into his father's, unsure of what the village was about. Mordecai could feel the magic in the air, a rough form to his way of thinking yet the swamp teemed with the essence of magic. He peered that the oozing sludge below the rocking wagon, uncertain as to why they had come to this place. Hud squeezed his hand back reassuring him. He carried the balance box with his right arm, hugged tight against his chest.

Halfway across the first bridge, shadows detached themselves from the huts strung along the intersections and stood, waiting for the party to join them on the landing. A raven cawed from the treetop and a monkey chattered a high pitched babble that announced their arrival as succinctly as a herald's trumpet.

A tall man stepped forward and gestured with one hand to a large communal hut on the far side of the swamp at the end of a curving boardwalk. "She is waiting for you, sire. Please follow me."

He turned and led them through the thickening swarms of bugs toward the entrance draped with a cloth woven with images of birds and snakes and fish. He drew aside the curtain and held it for them while they ducked through the opening.

Calleigh sat in a dark red chair of woven vines as thick as a thumb. The chair's twisted form was suspended from a looped chain of living vines that exited the hut through a hole in the roof. It looked to Mordecai like a child's swing in many ways and swayed gently as she leaned forward to see who approached from the doorway. Her eyes took in the men filing in the doorway and then she focused on Mordecai. She held out a gnarled hand. "Come to Calleigh, boy."

Mordecai approached Calleigh and took the proffered hand, hopping up onto her lap with a grin. She rocked the swing while the others watched. Hud took a half step but was stopped by the sharp look cast by Calleigh.

Caerwyn nodded his head in respect, as equals, but did not attempt to approach closer.

"So, child, what do you bring to Calleigh today?"

Mordecai shook the blanket-covered box and grinned. "It's a balance box, Calleigh, and I know how it works!" he said proudly, puffing out his chest.

"Do you? Well aren't you a brilliant one! Tell Calleigh. What does it do?"

"It balances the forces of good and evil at a spiritual level. It brings the world into harmony by restricting what will not balance, both good and evil."

"Very good!" she said, clapping her hands together, a big smile crinkling her cheeks. "And what happens if one tries to exert their will on the box?"

"It will entrap them within the box."

"Correct. So what was the original purpose of the box? Why was it created?"

"To heal the land and the people. To give them a way to correct the imbalances caused by greed in the world. It is also to give the mortal rulers a place to come and create peace between peoples. The box will right an imbalance both physically and spiritually."

"You are very wise for one so young, Mordecai. Calleigh is pleased. The king is wise to trust you with it." She raised her head to look Caerwyn directly in the eye.

"Step forward and petition Calleigh, son of Morpheus."

Caerwyn strode forward and bowed to the witch and then straightened.

"What is it you wish to ask of Calleigh? Speak the truth in your heart, as has this child."

Caerwyn cleared his throat then met her eyes once again.

"I come to ask your assistance and guidance. Your foresight is legendary. I ask that you to look into the future and what it holds. There is an ill breeze blowing. You must have felt it too? Alfreda and her people rode to the very gates of Cathair to bring warning of the trouble brewing along the border between my realm and the Primordial lands. It centers on the Highland Spine, and a foul smoke that stings the eyes and clogs the throat is rising from the peaks. If I am to be successful in curbing the unrest I need to know what is causing the smoke. Scouting parties return and report that mountain is erupting where volcanos never existed and periodic earthquakes shake the earth. Alfreda's people are being hurt, and some have died as a result of the eruptions."

Calleigh shifted in her chair, her wandering right eye struggling to focus on Caerwyn. "Calleigh can see the truth of the matter, but it may not help you, son of Morpheus."

Caerwyn frowned. "The truth is always useful. How can it not help? The Primordial are a superstitious people. They see signs and portends in the mountain's activity. They are rightly nervous and suspicious and interpret the eruptions as a sign of the god's displeasure."

Meanwhile, in Cathair, despite our assurances, the people of the kingdom spread rumours of Primordial tribes sneaking through the hills, snatching the unwary and performing rituals that are known only to their societies. Alfreda refuses to speak of the religious factions within the Primordial tribes, as the sacred rituals are not for outsiders to know or witness. Rumours and fear are fracturing the fragile peace between our peoples. Events are spiralling out of our control. We are on the verge of outright war. Alfreda swears that her people are not behind it, but I need to know the truth of the matter."

Calleigh closed her eyes, and silence descended. A lone tear leaked from the corner of her eye, tracing a bumpy path over the careworn wrinkles of her cheek. Mordecai reached up and softly wiped the tear away.

When she opened her mouth to speak it was barely a whisper, as though she were afraid to speak the words aloud. Softly, she murmured, "Calleigh knows that the answer is within you, Caerwyn. The people are both right and wrong. A terrible cataclysm is set to erupt and the godlings are central to it. Calleigh's Seeing Eye sees two paths set before you.

"On one path, world is swallowed by a terrible darkness and shadow spreads across the earth. On this path is the end of all mortal life within three generations of this vision.

"On the other path, the gods cease to exist and so do the godlings. The magical world dies and passes into myth. The world is inhabited by mortal beings, and mortal beings alone with no chance of rebirth.

"You must choose. Calleigh does not know which path is the right one or if you will be successful, regardless of which path you choose. Calleigh does know that if you do not choose a path, the world will be plunged into chaos and wars will ravage it until all life is eradicated, both mortal and immortal. The land will be salted until no life can exist. Calleigh's, yours, theirs, all life will be eliminated for all time.

Caerwyn stepped back in shock, and swallowed heavily. "All life?" His hands shook and he struggled to control the trembling of his limbs. "Surely there is some other path? Something other than an either-or proposition? There must be something that can be done to preserve all the life forms that live on this world?"

Her eyes opened, glistening bright but steady and bored into him, weighing, judging. "The answer is within you," she whispered softly, "and you must find it. Calleigh can see nothing more than what she has told you. Calleigh gives you these words of her own free will, at no cost. They are Calleigh's gift in the hope that you will recognize the way when it is placed before you."

She straightened in her chair and then set Mordecai on his feet. He gave Calleigh a hug then patted her shoulder, before running back to his father. Calleigh's eyes followed his progress. "The child can help you. Of that, Calleigh is certain. But it is all I know. Go now, you do not have much time."

Chapter 12

Artio

THE CLEARING WAS EXACTLY as they had left it. The fog had cleared, and in its place a steady drizzle of rain soaked the freshly churned earth. Already new growth sprung from the settled ground, a fuzzy green carpet of soft grass.

Hand in hand Artio and Genii entered the clearing and paused at the lip, eyes roving over their creation. Three years they had worked on it, planning the cutting of the rock from the mountain side. For the three years prior to that, they had searched for the precise materials, as Calleigh had been very precise in the recipe to make such a thing happen.

She had given Genii into Artio's care, allowing the godling to take her precious son from the swamp. His life had been in danger, so she had struck a bargain for his care for all time.

Initially, Artio had been looking for a companion that could help her with her care of the celestial bodies, as it was a lonely vigil, but the humans around her were too short lived. When she'd found the young wizard, it had seemed like the perfect solution.

Of course, Calleigh was reluctant to let her son go and had to be persuaded that the odds of him achieving adulthood were slim. Most wizards and witches did not survive a journey past edge of the swamp, falling prey to the swamp's hold on their magic.

Their magic was bound to the swamp, and it was a rare wizard or witch that could leave it with their magic intact. Without their magic, they were physically and mentally weakened and susceptible to a magical cancer which infested the hollows where their magic had been, destroying any residual ability until senility crept into their minds and they surrendered and died.

But Artio had surrounded Genii's magic within her eternal sphere of influence and had been able to shield him from the effects of being isolated from the swamp. They had been together ever since. What she had not counted on was falling in love with the young man as he grew. He soon caught up with her, in mental age if not in exact years, and she planned to increase his life span, as they appeared to be exactly the same age and would be forever more.

So Artio had visited Calleigh once more, when Genii was sixteen, and this time, with him in tow, to receive her blessing and her assistance in not only preserving his life but in making him as close to immortal as it was possible for a human to be.

And now, seven years later, they stood on the cusp of the fulfillment of that dream, to bind their souls to each other for all eternity.

Artio ran down the slope, her cape flapping around her shoulders, to the very center of the clearing. A broad whitish disc sat in the center of the circle of stones, and in its center a shallow basin was scooped out. Around the bowl, partially completed carvings were etched, runes of magic and spirit, taught to them by Calleigh. She had made them practice over and over and over, until they could carve them precisely. There could not be a line out of place.

The first set had allowed for the healing of the people. They had triggered the medicine wheel of the stones, a vital function, as the transformation to a near god would bring Genii to the edge of death. Without the healing of the medicine wheel, the absorption of the moon's energy would sear him to a crisp before he could be transformed by the moon. A careful balance between healing and absorption, aided by the potion, must be maintained or all would be for naught...and the runes were the trigger.

Genii joined her, and despite the rain, they set to work. Genii withdrew a leather-wrapped pouch from inside his cloak and flipped it open, extracting two chisels and two small hammers. He handed one set to Artio and he took the other and they set to work, chiselling the hard stone until the grey light failed them. As they worked, Genii's magic flowed into the stone and the lines glowed as they chiseled, the flow of magic sealing itself into the figure. The rock warmed and the light rain made a hissing sound as it evaporated on the heated surface.

As night descended, the ability to see accurately lessened. Fearful of making a mistake, they quit for the evening, retiring to the shelter of a crystal cave located through a rift of rock at the far end of the meadow. The cave had been their temporary home for the last year, and they had been overseeing the construction of the circle from it.

They lit the fireplace set against one wall and pulled provisions from a hollow shelf in the rock wall to eat. A kettle of water was placed on the hook over the fire, and Artio tossed some tea leaves into the water. They did not speak, content to enjoy the peace of their surroundings and weary from the day's work. As they sat near the warming fire, the light reflected off several thin glass vials, perched on a high shelf. A shimmer of magic surrounded the potions.

Three days. They had three days to complete the runes. Three days.

Chapter 13

Alfreda

THE PERSISTENT RAIN chased them down the Cathair road, the great cat that was Alfreda's mount yowling with displeasure about the mud clinging to her paws.

The battering mammoths, on the other hand, placidly plodded along the grassy roadsides, the divisions of their toes splayed like toes to counterbalance the slip and slide of the soil beneath their enormous feet. They left large flat discs behind them, which would dry to stepping stones of clay once warmed by the sun. Occasionally, they dipped their heads, dragging a tusk through the grasses and snagging a mouthful of the tender shoots, munching as they lumbered along.

Alfreda pulled her hood up higher and spread the cloak over her knees and down the back of the sabretooth to help keep him dry. The cat disliked travelling in any form of rain but did so at her command.

As she raised her head from the adjustment of her clothing, she saw a scout riding swiftly toward her. The captain of her forces peeled away from the head of one column and rode back toward her, intercepting the scout. Then, together they rode toward her position.

The scout's horse was lathered with sweat from the hard ride, despite the rain, nostrils flared wide as it sucked in air. It tossed its head as it was pulled to a halt in front of the great cat. The sabretooth paused, tail flicking, eyes narrowed at the snorting beast. The horse noticed the cat at the last minute and shied, nearly unseating its rider.

"My lady!" the scout said, recovering his balance. "I bring you grave news. There is a large Primordial force about twenty miles ahead. The flesh clans are on the move! They look to be headed toward Cathair."

"Toward Cathair?" she said sharply. "Are you sure?"

"Yes, my lady! I would put their numbers at two thousand strong, and they have a high priest with them!"

"High priest? Which one?" The scout shrugged, and Alfreda's frown turned into a scowl. "How dare they move onto this soil without my express permission! Return and bring this high priest to me, immediately! This is my command and so it shall be."

Captain Enyeto cleared his throat. Alfreda's eyes slid over to meet his grey ones. "You have something to add, Captain?"

He nodded. "The location of such a parley should be neutral. It is too great a risk to bring the two clans in close proximity. May I suggest we pick a location and invite them to meet with us? There is a good place about a day's ride from here, a natural amphitheatre. Command that they bring no more than three Primordial, including the high priest, and we do the same. Any accompanying guards must be left behind half a league from the meeting location."

"Excellent suggestion." Alfreda turned back to the scout. "Take these words to the high priest." As he made to turn away, she grabbed the scout's sleeve "Tell them, that if they fail to appear, I will be *sorely displeased.*"

The scout nodded and raced away.

Captain Enyeto tugged on his reins and dropped in beside Alfreda. His hand wandered to his mustache and he smoothed it with two fingers, a nervous habit of his especially when he feared his words were bound to be contentious.

He cleared his throat. With a rumbling catch in his voice, he said, "They can be here for only one reason, my lady. They are here to appease the silence of the gods. They are here to find a sacrifice."

"Ridiculous. I have forbidden it." She tightened her knees, squeezing harder than she intended and the cat quickened his pace, so that Alfreda jumped ahead of the captain.

He urged his mount forward and parallel to hers once again. "They cannot be allowed to roam the land. It would be an act of war against Cathair, and especially if they start taking human sacrifices."

Alfreda scowled at her captain but did not answer.

"Negotiation will fail, and every step they take into the country will escalate the tensions. There is only one solution. They must join their will to ours and submit their high priest as a token of peace."

"They will refuse to give up their high priest! He is sacrosanct. No one may touch a priest."

"Exactly...that is why we must take him while he sleeps."

"What do you propose?"

"We kidnap him. If we control the priest, we control the army."

She shook her head "It's too dangerous. He will be heavily guarded."

"Then he must be assassinated."

"*What*?"

"If he is dead, the reason for coming here is gone."

"Temporarily, yes, but at what cost? Do you really think they will not seek revenge?"

"Pardon, my lady, but isn't it part of the ritual of the high priests to have their people drink of the blood of the sacrifice to bind them to the priest?"

She nodded, staring straight ahead.

"Then you must strike the snake in the head to kill the body. Anything else is giving license. My lady." He ducked his head in respect.

They rode in silence for a while, the persistent drizzle obscuring her view of the battering mammoths by the roadside. Alfreda sighed and adjusted her hood when a drip splashed onto her nose. She sighed again, and then the hood turned slightly.

"Set it up. I do not want to know the details." The hood straightened, and she nudged her cat into a lope, leaving her captain behind.

Chapter 14

Helga

HELGA SKIRTED AROUND the splashing waters of Thunder Falls, anxious to get away from the cold mist rolling off the surface of the pool at its base. She clutched the satchel with the precious potion to her breast, afraid that she might drop it in a sudden slip on the damp path.

The mouth of her cave, disguised by a ribbon of water from the falls, parted as she approached. She passed through the waters untouched and into her fortress home.

She had chosen the location deliberately, as the falls masked the sounds of her experiments and other than the occasional Primordial pilgrim no one came to the remote location. She was able, therefore, to conduct her research without needing to constantly fend off intruders.

And now as she entered the cave, an unnatural heat met her. She smiled as the warm air enveloped her, chasing away the chill. The damp and musty cave smells of living underground also faded away. She placed the palm of her hand on a rune, cast into stone just inside the entrance, and a glowing strip of light as bright as a window to the outside world appeared down the center of the ceiling. A tunnel resembling a hallway was revealed. She walked down the smoothed stone floor following its natural twists and turns until it emptied into a cavern, open to the sky.

A railing of chiseled stone steered to the left to a stone staircase that clung to the side of the cavern, spiralling down on a gentle incline around the circumference of the walls until it spilled out onto the cavern floor. The walls faded from grey to a glossy black, the pumice stone giving way to smoothed obsidian.

Great curls of smoke twisted and rose from a deep pit that glowed ruby with the reflected light of lava, flowing at great speed past the breach, a great underground river of flame.

Helga glided down the curving staircase, intent on her destination. As she entered the lower half of her descent, her image danced across the dark mirror and she studied her reflection out of the corner of her eye as it slid across the glassy surface. Tall and slender of build, she knew that she was by far the most beautiful of the godling sisters. *My radiance should not be dimmed. Soon the world will acknowledge me as the supreme godling, or they will perish. I will have their obedience in life or their souls in death. Either way, they are mine. My dear brother, Caerwyn, will kneel to me before the solstice is finished or he will die, forever.*

At the base of the cavern, she walked across the pitted surface, her destination a tunnel in the far wall. Before she reached the dark smudge, the smudge moved and hooded figures detached themselves from the wall, sliding forward to hover a few paces from the wall. The

Charun bowed its head in acknowledgement of its mistress and then glided over to her side.

"What is your command, my mistress?" it hissed, the sound of its voice the rasp of a file. The sound raised a shiver along Helga's spine, a delicious shiver of anticipation. A second Charun slid out from a crack and followed the first. As Helga reached the opening, three more joined the first two, drifting along impossibly above the floor.

The Charun looked identical, except for the one who spoke. A circle glowed in the middle of its forehead. Tattooed between its eyes was a rune, the image a golden sickle blade on a sea of blood. The circle dripped between the deep ridges as the Charun's face crinkled the leathery grey reptilian skin reptilian of its brow.

"Time grows short. The solstice approaches and Artio has erected healing stones. This will undo all our hard work. The animal souls we have been enslaving may be snatched away from us before we can complete the circle. Come!" she snapped "We must make final preparations."

She entered the tunnel and with a snap of her fingers, a compressed ball of flame flickered to life to float over her outstretched palm, lighting the path for her feet. She strode along at a pace just short of a run, skipping down the stairs with light steps. The staircase wound down and around and twisted this way and that but finally leveled out and into the rock. After about a half hour of walking, it spilled out into a long cave split down the middle by a giant fissure. A ribbon of lava slipped along its course, flowing swiftly by and tumbled in molten splashes down into a widening pool at the end, which eventually breached into a waterfall of lava. Intense heat and foul fumes rolled and twisted against the ceiling, which stretched so far above that it could not be seen. Yet Helga knew that a thin crack carried the roiling smoke into the cavern above and eventually out a natural chimney to the mountaintop.

At the edge of the lava pool several more Charun lined up by the razor sharp edge, dipping ladles into the river of molten rock and then carrying them, one by one, to a raised platform. A mould stood three stories high with scaffolding and ramps allowing the Charun to float up the ramps unimpeded to the lip of the mould.

The mould resembled a large bull seated on its haunches. The nose was pierced with a golden ring and long horns ending in barbed points curled from its massive face. In its front hooves, it held a large golden scythe, the flickering light of the lava flashing across the surface of the blade. The mouth was open in a frozen snarl, its eyes glimmering sky blue as though alive. The darting eyes followed the movements of the Charun and then flickered over Helga's approach. She shivered at the intelligence reflected in those eyes, the soulful depths swimming in the rounded orbs.

Of course, there is intelligence. How could there not be? Even the lowest beasts have some form of intelligence. Trapped intelligence. Stolen souls enslaved to my will...and now they will become my greatest weapon.

She climbed the ramp and circled around until she could look down into the seemingly bottomless vessel, craning her neck to see over the rim. She reached inside her cloak and pulled out the precious vial of potion. She unstoppered the bottle, staring at the shimmering liquid. Then, with a flick of the wrist, swallowed half of the contents. The other half she tipped into the vessel where, it hissed upon meeting the lava. The bluish haze writhed and twisted in the potions vapour and a keening wail echoed up from the depths and then faded away.

Helga turned and started down the ramp but then stumbled as a piercing cramp rippled across her abdomen, doubling her over in pain. She sucked in a breath, forcing herself to straighten, her hand gripping the stone wall. The Charun by her side flicked its forked tongue across its teeth, sensing her weakness, tasting the air.

Helga pushed off the wall and walked forward, back straight and head held high. She dared not show any weakness around the Charun.

Her vision blurred and she swiped the back of her quivering hand across her eyes, attempting to clear them, to no avail. The fog obscured her vision, and a cold sweat broke out on her upper lip. She ran a hand along the inner wall of the scaffolding, feeling her way to the base, blinking frantically to clear her vision.

The potion...the binding goes both ways. I...must...dominate!

"*You **will** submit your will to mine! **I am the master!**"* she thundered silently.

Mentally, she stiffened her mind, forcing the mist to obey. She bore down on the silent collective, pressing her will against the hundreds of souls battering against the walls of her mind and slowly melded them, merging them into the core of her own soul.

She lifted her head, eyes clearing, to find a Charun reaching for her, slimy hands stretching for her throat.

Helga lifted a hand and out shot a brilliant white torch of flame that encompassed the Charun. It screamed a high keening wail that rose in pitch as the flames encompassed it, head to hem. With a burst of stars, the Charun exploded and vanished as if it never existed.

Helga whirled, ready to cast another comet of light at the other Charun, but they retreated into the shadows, melting away into the darkness, until hers was the only living soul remaining in the hot cavern. She knew they would return; they were bonded to this task.

Unsteadily, she left the cavern. *I will rest and assimilate the bond. I must be ready. Time is already too short.*

Chapter 15

Artio

"I THINK YOU SHOULD ask Helga."

Genii shook his head, negating the idea, crossing muscular arms across his chest in emphasis. "I don't think Helga would be interested. You saw her the other day. She left as soon as she could. She has no interest in the healing circle or how it works. She certainly doesn't wish to assist."

The medicine wheel, while not technically a wheel, still functioned as one. The wheel that best illustrated its operation was actually a spinning wheel. As it wove the spirit of the gods into a thread of healing, a godling could then take that thread and make a blanket of healing for all those within the circle. No form of healing was too complex. The wheel simply wove the right cloth for the healing required.

Medicine wheels were tricky to create and a gift of the gods. A large percentage of the wheel's operations directly tied in to the flow of spirit that came from the gods, which had been dwindling lately due to the decrease in prayers being offered to them. It was rare for a human to possess the kind of faith needed to power a medicine wheel. The Primordial high priests and high priestesses came close, but even they struggled to maintain a constant flow of spirit through the wheel.

The conversation was a sore spot between them. Genii was firmly of the belief that the further they stayed away from Helga, the better the eventual outcome would be. Something about Artio's sister made him uneasy, and he was reluctant to ignore what made him uneasy. It had kept him alive in the swamp and in the world since leaving the place of his birth.

"We do not need Helga's help. The focus is precisely set." He held up his hands as Artio opened her mouth to speak, halting her response. "Listen, the tremors will stop. The mountain always quiets in time. What could she possibly do that could stop it? Volcanoes are a part of nature."

"Yes, but these are not *natural*. You know this, as well as I do, Genii! You were the first one to note the pattern of the fire fall. She must have some idea of why the eruptions are increasing."

"There is no time. The solstice is tomorrow. By tomorrow evening, we must have the stones perfectly aligned. There is only time left to align them, not to research the why of their shifting. If we go chasing off after Helga right now, we will miss our window." He stepped up to Artio and enfolded her in his arms. "I do not want anything to spoil our plans. The alignment must be right. Perfect. Supreme." He bent his head and kissed her, silencing her protests. The sweetness of the kiss erased all complaint and discussion and when he lifted his head, she sighed and laid her ear over his beating heart. She would go along with his plans, but still the thought niggled in the back of her mind, that they were missing something...something important.

The disk in the center of the circle was now surrounded by a broader circle of crushed willow bark. Foxglove bloomed in tall stalks, and monkshood and mugwart was interspaced here and there. Surrounding it all was a wall of faceted amethyst crystals a full span high, fencing in the herbs which had been carefully gathered from the surrounding meadow to focus the plant energies within the medicine wheel.

All was prepared, except for the final adjustments.

They broke apart and returned to fine tuning of the stones. Genii took new measurements and with levers of stone, shifted the monoliths by fractional increments, so tiny as to be not visible to the naked eye. Genii and Artio worked long into the night, aligning the stones with the stars, the pale moon's reflection sliding over the creamy disk, a near perfect reflection on the smooth stone surface.

Tomorrow night, the moon would be full and perfectly aligned. All was ready.

They stepped back to admire their work. A slight breeze blew up the valley, smelling of sulphur. Genii shivered, but it was not from the cold of the breeze. The smell of an open grave rode the wind. He was being watched and his gaze was drawn to the tree line. A shrub shifted slightly, then stilled. He squinted at the brush, but nothing moved in the dark.

Chapter 16

Alfreda

ALFREDA APPROACHED THE ARRANGED meeting point above the amphitheatre, sliding off her great cat and scratching it behind her tufted ears. With a rumbling purr, the cat sank to the ground and cleaned her paws, great tongue rasping against the pads between her toes.

Two of Alfreda's captains stepped up beside her, short swords in both hands, drawn from harnesses strapped across their chests. They peered warily around at the surrounding tall grasses, but there was no hint that anyone had crossed this portion of land recently. The stalks were tall and unbroken, waving lazily as they passed.

The main body of warriors remained on the main road and three of them crossed the grassy plain. Flat and level, not a tree broke the horizon so they were on top of the dip of land before they saw it. The amphitheatre was a large natural depression in the plain, as though the gods had scooped up a large handful of clay for some purpose known only in celestial circles.

They had been preceded by the assassins sent ahead by Captain Enyeto. Alfreda sucked in a nervous breath as the rim of the bowl dropped away.

At their appearance, a great cloud of ravens burst from the floor of the amphitheatre, flapping and cawing and circling their prey. Captain Enyeto pulled an arrow from his quiver. With an economy of movement, he stroked the arrow to string and loosed. The first arrow was followed by another and another, falling amongst the birds and never missing a shot. Wounded birds flapped and cawed and were set upon by the other ravens, pecking and slashing with razor sharp beaks. In between the flapping and cawing, Alfreda glimpsed the bodies of the assassins, bloodied and unidentifiable except by the remnants of the clothing they wore. Of the high priest, she saw no sign.

Alfreda backed away from the rim and swallowed heavily, striving to not vomit at the smells now wafting out of the bowl on the stirred air. She hurried back to her cat and buried her face in its soft fur.

Captain Enyeto continued to kill the ravens until most were dead and the balance decided that the meal could wait and winged away over the plain with indignant squawks. Several long minutes passed while the Captains went down into the bowl to inspect the scene.

"They died quickly as far as we can tell." Captain Enyeto kept his eyes averted from her grief, not wanting to intrude on her privacy.

Alfreda gave a start at the sound of his voice and lifted her head from the great cat. She could taste the despair on the air, a tugging at her soul that told the real story, at least from the viewpoint of the deceased. Surprise and denial, pain and fear swirled through the air. Assassins they may have been for this particular venture, but at heart, they were Primordial souls and not evil in nature. Although normally this was Caerwyn's duty, she gathered their scattered essence and sent them on their way to her brother's care.

"What of the priest?" Alfreda asked, her voice harsher than she intended.

"I am sorry, my lady, but she appears to have disappeared."

"*She? A high priestess? How do you know?*" Alfreda asked sharply. Frowning, she reached out with her senses, searching for the woman and the path she had taken away from the meeting location. She could not sense her presence in the area.

"They were killed with this." Captain Enyeto opened his gloved hand to display an empty vial. "They were poisoned, my lady, and that is a woman's method. Men are much more brutal." Alfreda reached over and plucked the vial from his hand. "Be careful, my lady!" he protested "We do not know what kind of poison it is. It could be absorbed through the skin."

Alfreda grimaced and dropped the vial back onto his outstretched palm. "I do not remember the flesh clans having a high priestess. They have always worked with the male lineage. Why would they suddenly appoint a high priestess to this task? It makes no sense. They have always sent a male to the temple for the choosing."

"Yes, but has a male ever been chosen?" he asked.

"No, not as a temple priest. This has been a major part of the discontent between the two clan factions." Alfreda paced the floor with short strides, considering the puzzle. "They have not been silent regarding their displeasure, but there can be no accommodation for the sacrificial rituals they practice under the guise of appeasement of the gods. They refuse all requests from the spirit clan chiefs to attend their ceremonies, zealously guarding their secrets. Rare is the opportunity to observe or participate in their ceremonies. They are very much a closed society, and the only people who are allowed to enter their realm are those who have partaken in their ceremonies and become one of the tribe."

"I have heard that the joining ceremony involves the consumption of human flesh and blood?" Captain Enyeto grimaced at the horrid image, unconsciously gripping the hilt of his sword as though by pulling it out, he could slay the offending thought.

"Yes." Alfreda walked in a widening circle around them questing with her mind, searching once again for the illusive high priestess. She rubbed at a mosquito bite on her arm, smearing a little blood in the process. Frustrated, she hurried back to her mount and climbed back into her saddle. The great cat stretched and stood, tail twitching, and sniffed the air head swinging to the right to stare and then back in the direction of the amphitheatre. The ravens circled overhead and dived low and disappeared into the bowl with their departure.

"Let's rejoin our forces. We will march through the night. I want to join with the Kingsmen by dawn. I sense that Caerwyn is in danger. I must catch up with him quickly."

They galloped off towards the waiting Primordial hoard and reaching the head of the column, set a brisk pace for Daimon Ford.

Dark eyes watched their hurried departure, cloaked in robes that absorbed the background image and bent the light so that the eye slid right past. Standing close enough to hear every word, the cloaked figure chuckled. The narrowed eyes followed Alfreda, then dropped to the hand in front of its face and smiled. It was holding a needle and the needle was dripping with blood.

Alfreda's blood.

Chapter 17

Caerwyn

THE JOURNEY OUT OF THE SWAMP was a long and arduous one, filled with buzzing insects and biting flies, but worst of all, were the tall broad-leafed plants that blocked their passage. Every branch was covered with fine, transparent hairs that hung from the stems like moss, but it was unlike any moss Caerwyn had ever seen.

The fragile strands drifted in the currents of air. Caerwyn swore they were hunting living beings. Attracted to motion, they would wind their tendrils around any creature that crossed their path, twisting in the breeze to float down onto an unsuspecting arm, softly wrapping itself around and around. Microscopic barbs set against the tug as the victim moved on, unaware of the plant's activities. The stinging vegetation went out of their way to slap up against flesh, and Caerwyn swore one plant was actually following them as they finally reached the edge of the swamp.

He did not need to encourage his men to keep going; they had no desire to linger within the confines of the swamp.

Three days and nights after their exit from the swamp brought the Kingsmen to the crest of a ridge. The River Erinn came into view, a ribbon of dark in a flattish flood plain, dotted with willow trees.

The last gasp of night faded before the blush of the predawn sun.

Caerwyn sat his Pegasus at the head of the assembled army, watching the approach of the warriors under Alfreda's watch. The spirit clan warriors moved with the precision of clockwork. Even the battering mammoths swaying gait kept rhythm with the marching clansmen.

Caerwyn could only see them from his vantage point because of the flickering torches held by the lead warriors. They crept out of the darkness of the southern plain, the moon long since set. It would be the better part of the day before they were able to merge their two forces and march on the mountain.

Caerwyn turned Brimstone back to face the mountain. A never-ceasing glow could be seen flickering on the side of the mountain near the summit. Smoke curled and twisted into the air, forming a dense mushroom-shaped cloud with a pink underbelly. Lightning flashed within the roiling smoke, and occasionally a bolt would stab down toward the rocky base.

Helga had planned her distraction well, for between himself and the fiery ledge, a Primordial host stood, watching their approach. He grimaced with distaste. Civil war...he had never wanted it to come to this.

He dug his heels into Brimstone's side and launched into the air.

* * *

From the banks of the ford of the River Erinn, the Primordial clan chief of the flesh tribes watched as the horizon resolved into a skyline thick with mounted Kingsmen. Vertical pikes broke the sky like the sharpened pole fences of a wooden fortress, stretching the entire width of the valley, from river to treeline. The Kingsmen were set six men deep with archers and swordsmen filling in the last two files. Heavy armour plate glinted off the bodies of the horses, reflecting the first rays of morning, refracting over the curvature of the earth.

A Kingsmen rode back and forth in front of the men, a long thin trumpet strung with the sky blue flag of the Royal house of Cathair along its length. Caerwyn lifted the trumpet and blew a long shivering blast on the horn as he galloped past the orderly rows. The front row snapped a salute as he passed, a sea of arms like the curl of a cresting wave.

The flesh clan chief, Akecheta, a necklace of neck bones decorating the front of his skins, sat astride his black and white paint, stroking its muscular neck, comforting the high-strung mountain-bred stallion. It snorted, catching the scent of the other horses across the valley, and whinnied with excitement.

The Primordial warriors, their barebacked mounts snorting and shuffling, crowded in around the clan chief and gestured toward the approaching army jabbering excitedly to one another.

"Enough!" Caerwyn roared, "Do you wish the enemy to see you flapping around like chickens with a fox in their midst? Do you want them to see us as *afraid*?" His dark glare made heads drop in shame, avoiding his hawkish gaze. "Daimon be praised," he spat. "Cease this babbling! Rein in your mounts!"

The milling warriors stilled their horses, forming a loose row facing the intruders and the murmuring ceased. The clan chief rode in front then circled behind the outnumbered clansmen, his stallion snapping at the other horses as he passed. He scanned their heavily painted faces, searching for any trace of fear. No warrior would admit to it. Fear was for the weak, and the penalty was death. Painted onto the skin of some were crude depictions of creatures thought to reside in the underworld. Others wore Daimon masks decorated with glowing charcoal eyes that granted a flickering life to the fierce images. Every warrior brought their spirit guardian to battle; none would dare fight without their protection this day. Today they would face Kingsmen and kin, cousins who called the traitorous spirit tribes home.

A gust of wind roared down the mountainside and gusted out onto the plain, hot and sulphur-scented. It burned the nostrils and coughing broke out in the ranks. It sped past the flesh clan warriors and eyes watered in its wake. Akecheta wheeled around to stare at the mountain, scowling at the source of the offending wind. The mountain rumbled and the cloud of smoke flashed as an eruption of rock and lava spewed from the rent in its side. Boulders of rock shot into the air and sailed in a slow arch past his warriors and out into the plain. The mounted Kingsmen shouted a warning, and their lines were abruptly broken as men and horses dodged the flaming missiles landing amongst their ranks.

Cheers rose from the Primordial warriors and shouts of glee as the mountain continued to spew its fiery belly skyward. Small fires sprung up, burning across the grassy plain, and smoke drifted across the parched surface, spreading quickly. A wall of fire created a barrier between the enemy armies.

"Daimon be praised!" shouted the flesh clan fighters. "Our guardians go before us!"

"The Gods are pleased!" shouted another.

"Victory will be ours!"

"Honour to the high priests! They show us the will of the Gods!"

There was no fear in their eyes now; their faith renewed, they faced the enemy boldly. Assurance that victory would be theirs gleamed in every painted face.

* * *

Caerwyn felt the shock wave from the explosion before he heard it, but it was the projectiles of pumice and ash that drew his eyes as balls of fire roared out from the missing face of the mountain crater.

Brimstone screamed and attempted to dodge the flaming bullets but several tore into his wing, puncturing it, others burning along hip and flank. Caerwyn struggled to steer his panicking mount to the west, but the fiery debris rained down on them as the mountain continued to belch. His eyes watered with the acrid smoke. As he cleared his vision, he spied a hollow tucked in against the base of the mountain. Brimstone tumbled toward the surface, and Caerwyn sawed on the reins to steer him toward what was the only sanctuary in sight. The ground rushed up toward him, and at this speed, even he could be killed if he were to make impact with the ground. Caerwyn kicked his feet free of the stirrups and slid further back on his saddle, readying himself to jump at the last second.

A sizzling pellet sliced across Brimstone's cheek and tore through the main muscle of the wing, which folded under the combined weight of Brimstone and Caerwyn. The Pegasus spun around and around, a maple leaf tossed in the wind. With a crash, the Pegasus struck the ground and rolled, a tangle of wings and mane and tail, tossing Caerwyn over his back. He flew through the air and his head smacked hard against an upright grey stone pillar. Bright stars popped across his vision, and he knew no more.

Chapter 18

Mordecai

MORDECAI STOOD UP on the seat of the wagon, peering toward the mountain. Great plumes of smoke rose from its crest, and fiery breaches could be seen in the stone façade despite the dark that clung to the mountainside in the late afternoon sun. It wasn't the roaring mountain that drew his eye. Below the summit, partway down the mountainside a nimbus glowed, a flattish blue aura that was neither cloud nor smoke. Brighter than the rock face, it throbbed with light and life.

"Father, what is that place?" he asked.

Hud followed his son's pointed finger, but his eyes were not as keen as Mordecai's. *Or what he is looking at, is magical,* he thought.

"What is it you see? I see the mountain erupting and lots of clouds and smoke."

"Do you see that blue disk? It sits there, just above that outcropping of pinkish rock." He stared at the spot his lips pursed, hand still pointing in the direction of his gaze.

Hud shook his head. "I'm sorry Son, but I cannot see it. Why do you ask?"

"Because that is where I need to be. Can you take me there?"

"It is behind the Primordial lines. How do you expect us to get there?"

"We can fly. The king brought extra Pegasus." Mordecai pointed to a snowy white Pegasus grazing alongside three other Pegasus at the rear of the Kingsmen. "Her name is Moonbeam. That is her true name. She told me." He grinned and pushed the blanket-covered box to the edge of the floor before hopping down from the wagon. Grabbing the box, Mordecai ran over to the Pegasus. "She told me I could ride her."

Hud jumped down from the wagon and followed his son over to the Pegasus. Moonbeam lifted her slim head and chewed a mouth full of grass, eyeing their approach. She snorted and flapped her wings then settled them against her sides and went back to grazing.

Behind Moonbeam, a great cat bounded through the grass, a woman on her back. Hud raised his hand in greeting. "My lady!" he said and bowed low.

"Cinda!" cried Mordecai, as Alfreda rode up to the pair of them. She halted the cat short of the Pegasus and slid to the ground then hurried over to the pair of them.

"Where is Caerwyn?" she said anxiously, eyes searching the area for her brother.

"He is in the air with Brimstone," Hud said, alarmed at the frantic look on her face. "Why? Is something wrong?"

"Yes, he is in danger, and I cannot reach him. He is not answering my summons. Something is definitely wrong!"

"We must search for him then. The only ones who could find Brimstone are the Pegasuses. We were going to take Moonbeam here and go check out an area by the mountain that has caught Mordecai's attention."

"I will join you then." Alfreda turned around and spied a third, toffee-coloured Pegasus. "I will ride Sandstorm."

"Somehow, it seems appropriate to ride a Sandstorm and Moonbeam to search for elusive Brimstone. It could get hot before we are finished." Hud flashed a crooked smile, amused.

Alfreda gave him a weak smiled in return. Cinda nudged Alfreda's arm, and she yowled, complaining about the change in plans. Her tail twitched and her golden eyes narrowed at the commotion around her, ears twitching. "Not this time, Cinda. I must fly!" Cinda rubbed up against Alfreda and then rolled onto her side, begging a bell scratch. Smiling weakly, Alfreda scratched her soft belly, and straightened.

Mordecai was already scrambling onto the back of Moonbeam. "So what are you waiting for?" he called "Let's get going!"

Hud pulled himself up behind his son and Alfreda caught up Sandstorm and swung onto his back. With a heel to flank, the Pegasuses launched into the air, wings sweeping quick beats to carry them skyward. The ground shrank away and the men shrank to the size of wooden toys. With swift strokes, the Pegasus pulled higher into the sky then leveled off to coast on an updraft from the mountain. The wind was thick with a foul stench that made their eyes water and made them tuck their faces in against their sleeves.

With a roar, the mountain exploded and great chunks of flaming debris arced across the sky, raining down on the troops below. Kingsmen fell like dominos, dodging the deadly missiles.

Hud was suddenly thankful for the height that the Pegasus had climbed to, as they now flew above the debris field, but the wind became white hot, the erupting mountain super-heating the air. Whirlwinds of flame created violent updrafts and downdrafts that sucked at the Pegasus, who struggled to not be pulled into the flaming trailers in the sky.

Mordecai pulled ahead of Alfreda on Moonbeam, intent on the location only he could see. She put Sandstorm nose to tail with Moonbeam, and together they swept toward the bubbling mountainside.

As they crossed over the Primordial forces, faces turned upward and arms pointed and an arrow or two was loosed in their direction, but they fell short and tumbled back to earth. Alfreda looked back over her shoulder, searching the clan for the high priest...or high priestess if that was who was truly in charge...but she could not pick out anyone to fit that description in the crowd of clansmen.

They crossed the River Erinn. Once on the north side of the river, the buffeting winds ceased and they were able to descend through the caustic smoke, coughing and holding their sleeves over their noses through the dense vapours. The heat tore at their throats and scorched the exposed skin on their faces.

The hair on Hud's skull rose. *I wonder if it will burst into flame.*

They passed through the cloud.

"There it is!" shouted Mordecai. He urged Moonbeam on toward what now appeared to be a crater on the mountainside. A blue aura hung over the tree-lined clearing. In the center, large upright stones formed a circle from which the blue mist emanated.

The Pegasuses dropped lower, and one by one they landed in the far end of the clearing, knee-deep in the meadow grass. A whicker came from the long shadows reaching half way across with the setting of the sun. Brimstone stepped forward from the shadow, limping, wings dragging on the ground.

With a gasp, Alfreda slid from Sandstorm's back and ran over to the injured Pegasus.

"Where is Caerwyn, Brimstone?" She edged around Brimstone, careful to not touch the deep burns running across his chest and flank. Brimstone rolled his eyes and bared his teeth in warning.

"Mordecai, Hud, go into the forest and gather some witch hazel. Quickly!"

"But, Alfreda, you need to know…" Mordecai broke off as gave him a push towards the woods. Hud grabbed Mordecai's hand and tugged him along behind him. They ran off up the path past the stones and disappeared into the woods.

Alfreda turned back to Brimstone. "Where is Caerwyn? Where is he, boy?" Alfreda opened her mind, searching for her brother. *Caerwyn, can you hear me?* Her mind quested, searching the link of the bond they shared, but was as if he had disappeared. A stone cold wall was the only sensation where normally there would be a tangled web of emotions.

Alfreda turned on the spot, eyes searching the strange clearing. The stone placement was of recent date, the stone freshly quarried, and the soils around it showing recent activity. In the broad circle, several rings narrowed to focus on a white disk. She frowned and took a step toward the rune-covered stones. *Artio, this is your handiwork, isn't it?*

At that moment, a shout echoed from the woods. "My lady, Alfreda, come quickly!" A shiver of apprehension slide down her back, but she did not need any further calls from Hud, Caerwyn's silence was all the excuse she needed. She hiked up her skirts and ran for the path into the trees.

Alfreda pushed through the scrub brush and into the forest, following Hud's call, but the forest was dark with the descent of night. She stumbled down the path. As she leapt over a thick root, slimy hands grabbed her arms. A cloth was shoved over her face, smelling strongly of petrol. She struggled to get it off her face, but her consciousness faded and she sagged limply in the Charun's hands. They turned as one and floated away into the woods.

Hud kept a hand clamped tightly over his son's mouth, the other arm around his waist, keeping him still and silent.

After several moments of silence, he relaxed his hold.

"The Queen!" Mordecai whimpered, and a big tear rolled down his cheek.

"You knew this was coming, Mordecai. You were the one who told me." His father wiped the tear off his cheek and pulled him onto his lap. "Yes, but I didn't *want* it to happen. I wish the box had been wrong." Another tear leaked out from under eyes squeezed tight.

"Caerwyn will understand. So will Alfreda. You must trust them." Mordecai nodded then buried his face in his father's chest and sobbed.

Chapter 19

Artio

ARTIO EXITED THE CAVE at the end of the meadow. As she straightened, she stopped so abruptly that Genii plowed into the back of her. He grabbed her around the waist to keep them both from toppling over.

"Pegasuses!" she breathed, watching the winged mounts. "Caerwyn is here somewhere." Her eyes scanned the clearing, but nothing stirred other than the Pegasus gorging on the lush grass.

The mountain rumbled, and her eyes were drawn to the summit towering above them. "The mountain grows restless. Whatever is happening inside that mountain is giving it a belly ache. I fear we will live to regret what that is."

"Come. The light fades. We must prepare."

Genii reached back inside the cave and pulled out a rucksack and slung it over his shoulder and followed Artio down the sloping pasture to the great circle of rock. The sun was already hidden behind the treetops and long fingers of shadow stretched to cover more than half of the clearing. Artio took the sack from Genii's hands and loosened the drawstrings and then reached inside to pull out the two lumps of moon rock. She handed them to Genii before reaching back inside and pulling out the collection of vials.

The first vial contained tiny grains of crushed diamond that sparkled in the low light. Artio crossed into the circle and knelt on the white circle then pulled the stopper and emptied the contents of the vial into the bowl. Genii then placed the two chunks of meteorite in the center of the diamonds.

Returning to the satchel, Artio removed the remaining two vials, both of them containing the purple elixir provided to them by Calleigh. A catalyst, she had called it, to enhance the spells cast.

Artio returned to Genii and gave him one of the vials. She sat on one side of the circle and he sat down opposite her, cross-legged, facing Artio, knees touching. The sun faded and the light of the day waned. As the clearing darkened, the bowl of diamond twinkled, seemingly lit from within. But the source of the light was the moonstones, which initially pulsed weakly but gained strength as the light faded.

Artio pulled the cork on her potion and drank it down in one and Genii copied her, tossing the empty vial away. He reached across to capture Artio's hands in his.

"Do not let go, no matter what happens, Genii," Artio instructed. "You should start to feel numb and may even doze off, but do not let go." Genii nodded, and Artio could already see his face slacken. "I will be here with you the entire time. Do not be afraid, my love." Genii's eyes drooped, but he did not slump. Rather, he seemed frozen, his knees and back locked in place, rigid.

Artio dropped her eyes to the moonstones and chanted an incantation of her own devising. The moonstone's pulsing quickened and so did Artio's heartbeats, excitement and the potion racing through her veins. Her eyes blurred and she entered a trance, continuing to spell the moon, pulling it to her, commanding it to obey her will. Her soul lifted from her body and entered the moonstone, her body locking just as rigidly as Genii's. The clearing, the ring of rune-rock, the moon circle all faded from conscious thought. There was nothing but the moon.

Chapter 20

Captains Collide

CAPTAIN ENYETO DIPPED HIS HEAD and pushed his way into the tent of Captain Brennan, followed closely by his Kingsmen guards, who looked appalled at the Primordial captain's boldness. They knew he was of Alfreda's clan, but even so, all Primordial looked the same to them.

Captain Brennan stood as Enyeto entered then waved his guards away. They bowed and exited the tent.

"Captain." Brennan nodded his head toward a makeshift bench placed on one side of a low table, inviting him to sit across from him.

As Enyeto lowered himself onto the bench, Brennan growled "Alfreda is missing too, I take it?"

"Yes, she left about four hours ago and has not returned. Night is falling. I fear they will not return this evening. I fear for their safety."

Brennan strode back and forth in the small confines of the tent, worrying the familiar groove in the carpet, a result of prior campaign pacing. "I am planning a night attack on the Primordial barring our way. Are your clansmen willing to go up against kin? I would prefer to negotiate, but such offerings have met deaf ears in the past and I see no reason for this to be any different. Nevertheless, I intend to send out a scout under a white truce flag to parley."

"My clansmen are as anxious as the Kingsmen to recover their queen. You would have to fight them also, to keep them from accompanying you. When will the truce flag be sent out?"

"He should be there now. Come let's see what kind of a reception he receives."

Brennan strode out of the tent, Enyeto on his heels. They strode past the infirmary tents where the wounded were being tended to. The moans of men in pain followed them as they passed by. "How many were injured?" Enyeto asked.

"About ten percent of my force. Twenty dead. It could have been worse."

Enyeto grimaced at the numbers.

A few minutes' brisk walk brought them to the closest lookout point. Grabbing a pair of looking glasses from the closest scouts, he climbed the rise, handing one to Enyeto.

The distant rider sprang close as they put the glass to eye, his flag whipping over his head from a pole set in a pocket by his stirrup. He was about one hundred paces from the lead row of Primordial clansmen when a hail of arrows arched out. Multiple arrows pierced his chest, and he fell sideways, dead before he hit the ground. His foot twisted in its stirrup and did not dislodge. His panicked mount snorted and wheeled around, racing back toward them, but a second hail made the horse stumble as arrows pierced its legs, and a final arrow in the neck severed the jugular and it collapsed in a skidding heap. When the dust settled neither rider nor horse moved a muscle.

Brennan swore loudly. "Well, that would be your answer, bloody Primordial heathens!"

Enyeto raised an angry fist and put it down on his thigh. "You will have to race me to the bastards, Captain. We will have first blood!" he snapped and wheeling around marched away toward his waiting escort. Five Primordial horsemen peeled away to race back to the spirit clan warriors. "Meet me on the field of battle in ten minutes."

"*To horse!*" roared Brennan and the scouts took off running to spread the word. His face darkened and all who saw him coming knew it was time. They would cross the River Erinn at Damion Ford or die trying.

Men spilled out of tents and doused cook fires, grabbing armour and belting it over tunics, stamping feet into boots. Within minutes, they were mounted and formed into their units, which peeled off to join up with similar stirrings of the spirit clan forces. They raced toward each other, then both armies curved to ride side by side, Kingsmen's horses matching the horses and great battering mammoth's pace for pace, stride for stride. The battering mammoths sensed the coming battle and bellowed a piercing blast so loud the riders to clap hands over their ears. The ground shook from the combined pounding of thousands of hooves, creating their own mini-earthquake, flattening the grass and churning the soil.

The flesh clans fanned out to face the oncoming rush screaming insults and waving fists clenching blades and wickedly curved scythes on long poles. Their leader rode down the long line in front of them, screaming wildly and carrying a pole from which dangled the head of a man, dripping blood as he passed by. The head swayed side to side and as he turned once again, the face flashed to the oncoming Kingsmen. The head of the scout who had fallen in the field not ten minutes ago. The flesh clans screamed in blood lust, eyes crazed behind devilish masks and as one, they surged out to meet the oncoming rush.

The gap closed swiftly and the battle commenced.

Overhead, a vulture circled lazily. It was quickly joined by others.

Chapter 21

Godlings

CAERWYN'S EYES FLUTTERED SLOWLY as he attempted to crawl out from under the fog of pain. His head thrummed as though stone masons were chipping away at his skull, the throb as sharp as a chisel. He clawed himself awake. As his eyes opened, his first sight was a ceiling of hand-hewn stone. The chamber danced with firelight. He turned his head and a wave of dizziness made the firelight jiggle, in a nauseating way.

He closed his eyes briefly. When he opened them again, he found himself face to face with a robed figure, eyes glowing within a deep hood and skeletal hands folded inside its sleeves. It floated above the surface of the floor.

Caerwyn made to sit up but found his hands were tied behind his back and a chain rattled on the ground. No matter. There was not a rope in the kingdom or in the world that could hold him. He tensed his muscles, straining to shred the bonds, but all that happened was a rattling of the chain as his muscles flexed. Surprised, he bent his head to look at what held him, but this brought another wave of dizziness on so intense that he barely resisted the urge to vomit.

The Charun hissed at him, "Be still. The mistress says you are to lay still."

Caerwyn rested his head back on the cold stone floor to cool his fevered brow. "Who is your mistress?" he asked, but he thought he knew. Only one person would choose to live here and only one could devise a way to restrain him. That knowledge was restricted to those with similar powers.

"She comes. She comes." The creature floated back, and from a doorway Caerwyn could not see before stepped Helga.

She paused in the doorway, silhouetted by a back lighting of her own making. "Hello, dear brother. So nice of you to drop in, but I must admit, you have slept far too long and unfortunately have overstayed your welcome." She descended the last step and strode over to stand in front of him, crossing her arms under her breasts.

"But now that you are here, what to do with you? You see, you really should ask permission before dropping in on me. I could be...busy."

"Helga, untie me, enough of this foolishness!"

"I am afraid I can't do that, not yet. I have plans for this evening. Until I am ready to leave, you will stay right here." She laughed as Caerwyn struggled with his bonds. "Don't worry. I will invite you to the party. Oh yes, I wouldn't want my sibling to miss the fun! Where is our lovely sister, Alfreda? She must be with you. You would think you two were twins, the way you copy each other. Never mind. I am sure she will make an appearance shortly. Either way, she does not have long to live. She seems to have run afoul of poison."

"Helga! Are you mad? Untie me!" She continued to ignore Caerwyn's struggles and he ceased trying to free himself, as the blackened ropes tightened painfully. Instead he demanded, "What is this all about? Are you behind the eruptions?"

Helga smiled, but it did not reach her eyes. "Alas, an unfortunate side effect, but I have made adjustments for it."

"Adjustments? To what?" He stared at her and a chill washed over him. "Helga, you haven't been drilling into the core of the earth, have you?"

Helga's smile widened, and she chuckled at the shock and fear that flashed through Caerwyn's eyes.

"Just a tiny experiment, Caerwyn. You would not understand. This is my realm." Her gaze hardened. "The time has come. I will not be sent the dribbles of humanity to rule. I will have my piece of the world...with or without you." She smiled at his expression. "Don't worry. You will get a front row seat, I promise!"

She spun on her heel and headed deeper into the cave. Caerwyn's eyes followed Helga, and it was then that he saw they were not alone. Hundreds of Charun crowded the cave. What he had originally taken for firelight was revealed to be a river of lava that split the cavern in two. About a dozen of the creatures milled around a tall something, carting containers of lava up a sloping ramp to the top and dumping it over the side. When the last of the Charun descended, the scaffolding collapsed to the ground with an ear-splitting clatter. A two-story tall idol was revealed, the casing glowing with the heat of the lava, but that was not what drew Caerwyn's gaze. The eyes glowed *blue* with intelligence. The idol had a *living soul* trapped within it, perhaps more than one. *Where did Helga find living souls? These souls are mine to care for. They should have returned to me!*

With a grunt, he was roughly rolled over and a canvas sack was pulled over his head. Hands pulled the rough chain from the loops on the floor, and he was dragged by his arms upright, his shoulders screaming in protest. Shoved from behind to get his feet going the desired direction, he stumbled on the rough surface. The same slimy hands lifted him to his feet, bony fingers wrapping around each bicep and Caerwyn felt the presence of death in their grasp.

The death of a godling was never contemplated, the thought foreign to him, but suddenly he knew it to be a real possibility.

Surely Helga would not go so far? Caerwyn thought, but he was unsure of anything anymore. The Charun did not let go of him, but held him tightly between them, his feet dangling in space as they floated him up the passageway.

By the change in temperature, Caerwyn knew they had risen above the level of the lava and into the natural coolness of a cave. Then, a freshening breeze announced the exit to the outside world. A waterfall met Caerwyn's ears and flora slapped against his feet as he floated along between the Charun. They did not speak but carried him silently along, to where he did not know.

Eventually they halted, lowering him to the ground. A pole bumped his back and the chain was dragged through another ring with a rattle, binding him to the pole. The canvas hood was not removed. Silence descended, unbroken by cricket or frog. Caerwyn attempted to scrub the hood off of his head, rubbing it up and down on the pole and it inched up a bit at a time until the sack was over his ears at the back. His head flopped forward and the sack fell off into his lap.

He raised his head and his mouth dropped open at the sight before him. He was tied to a pole at the base of a mammoth stone pillar, over two stories high. A circle of stone created a ring from which a fiery light flickered. In the center of the circle around a flat disk sat his sister, Artio and a man, both frozen in a trance, moonlight circling their still forms in ribbons of streaking light. Directly across the circle from him was Alfreda tied in a similar fashion to one the grey pillars of rock.

The Charun who had carried him to the stones melted away back up the path, and they were left completely alone. Silence fell, complete except for a faint hum at the center of the circle.

Weakly, Alfreda stared at Caerwyn across the expanse and their gazes locked. She was similarly bound, slumped against the pole. She shifted her position, and pain shot up her arm as she straightened. It was as if a poison raced through her veins. She could not feel the connection to her world anymore. Her talents were fading. *I'm sorry*, whispered Alfreda to Caerwyn's mind. *I failed to rescue you.*

It's not your fault. I was knocked out of the sky and hit my head. It knocked me unconscious. Helga captured me that way.

What is this place? What is wrong? You look horrible! he messaged.

It is a medicine wheel. I recognized it as soon as we landed in the clearing. I think it is Artio's construct, although I do not understand all of that, she nodded to the circle of light, *or what she is up to. What could she possibly intend to heal?*

Well, when that moon has fully risen, it will dump enough energy into this circle kill everyone within it, including you and me. Look at the runes, Alfreda. This is not good. What are we going to do?

Hud and Mordecai are with me. They fled when Helga attacked, and we were separated. They are still out there, somewhere. Mordecai is a smart boy. He will come up with something to save us.

Suddenly, a distant voice echoed in Caerwyn's ears, advice he had recently received and only now understood.

The answer is within you, she whispered softly, *and you must find it. Calleigh can see nothing more than what she has told you. Calleigh gives you these words of her own free will, at no cost. They are Calleigh's gift in the hope that you will recognize the way when it is placed before you.*

Caerwyn searched with his mind and found the boy huddled with his father in the shrubbery at the edge of the clearing. He pulled their consciences into the web of thought with his sister and spoke to the pair of them.

Mordecai, what is your plan? Do you have the balance box with you?

Chapter 22

Mordecai

THE BRUSH PARTED as Mordecai and Hud squeezed their hands between the branches, creating a small hole through which they could peer at the clearing before them.

The Charun slid past them, sweeping up the path at a much faster pace than they had gone down it, with Caerwyn suspended between them. Helga's summons of the Charun was paramount. Her command they instantly obeyed, and they left the clearing with no more regard for the prisoners than cattle in a feed lot.

Mordecai was glad for the Charun departing. They made his skin crawl. The magic needed to create them was highly sensitive and volatile, and their presence made his skin itch as though he had fallen in stinging nettle.

Suddenly, Mordecai felt the brush of a mind against his, a familiar touch. It was as if he prayed, his mind opening to the presence of God. His father gasped beside him as he felt a similar sensation, and then a voice filled their minds.

Mordecai, with the curiosity of a child and the knowledge of a wizard, easily replicated the form of contact, solidifying the connection.

I have my balance box right here beside me, sire. Mordecai's hand twitched to the box.

I know you have been working on its secrets, and I believe you have figured out how it works.

I have, sire. The box told me.

Caerwyn looked over at Alfreda and grimaced. "Time is short. Either you must free us immediately, and we take our chances on stopping whatever is going on here with no idea of what is about to happen, or we sit here and try to ride out the coming storm and attempt to fight from within. I believe either path spells disaster for the world. Calleigh's warning rings strongly in my ears."

"There is no time to come up with a third plan. Not by me, anyways, but I believe you have the third answer, that you have held it all along."

Caerwyn's head swivelled until he was looking directly at where the small boy hid. "Come to me, Mordecai," he commanded, and Mordecai and his father slid out from the brush and came down into the clearing. They approached the king, both kneeling before him on the grass, heads bowed. Once they were standing before him, Caerwyn spoke.

"Tell us why you have brought the balance box?"

Mordecai stared at his toes poking out of his dusty sandals. The silence stretched.

"Mordecai?" Alfreda's voice drifted across the space. "Do not be afraid. We will not be angry. Tell us what you know."

A fat tear slid down his cheek and it was soon followed by others. Hud hugged him close. "You both must die," he croaked. "It is the only way to stop them."

Silence greeted his words.

"Mordecai, come here, and you too, Hud," commanded Caerwyn.

"I cannot undo these bonds. They are magically forged. But I need to touch you. Help me to stand."

Hud put a hand under Caerwyn's elbow and helped him to his feet, sliding up the pole.

"Now, I want both of you to kneel behind me, under my hands."

They did as they were bidden. Caerwyn placed his hands on either side of Hud's head.

He closed his eyes and drew on his godling spirit and a blue flame sprang to light and enveloped Hud's head in its glow.

"From this day forward, you will be branded with the oak leaf, the royal seal of Cathair. You and your descendants, going forward, will be the royal house of Cathair. You are my heir and my chosen successor. From this day forward, you will be king." The cool blue flame pulsed and a tattoo of an oak leaf appeared briefly on Hud's cheeks and a permanent tattoo appeared on the inside of his right arm.

Caerwyn shifted his hands to Mordecai's small head and the blue flame flickered around him, brightening as it mixed with his wizard's magic. "Mordecai, you are hereby charged with the care of our souls, should the fate of the world demand the sacrifice. You shall hold our souls in your care for all eternity. You are commanded to guard the souls of all humanity and provide for their care in our absence. We place our very existence in your hands. You will be responsible for maintaining the balance of the world, and you will be the counterstroke to Helga's evil for all eternity. So I have commanded, so it shall be done!" Caerwyn shouted.

"So you have commanded, so it shall be done!" shouted Alfreda in confirmation.

The glow faded and Caerwyn slumped back to the ground, the spell tiring him.

Hud and Mordecai stood and came back around in front of Caerwyn and bowed to him. Caerwyn shook his head. "You do not bow to me, my friends. We are now equals."

Mordecai ran up and hugged him tight and then turned away and approached the circle where Artio and Genii sat frozen in time. The moonlight swirled, wisps of fog-like trails fading into the dark. Mordecai crept up to them, careful to not touch the fingers of moonlight, slid the balance box under the orb of light until it rested directly over the heart of circle. He backed carefully away and then ran over to Alfreda and hugged her tightly. She laid her cheek against his soft brown hair, murmuring softly to him.

Mordecai raised his head. The true moon glow increased swiftly as it slowly crested the edge of the clearing. The humming at the center of the stones rose in pitch.

"You must go now. Hurry! Remove yourself from this area. Stay clear of the danger. The future depends on you staying safe. Go, my friends, *go!*" yelled Alfreda.

Hud, with an anguished look at his former king, ran to Mordecai, grabbed his outstretched hand, and bolted for the Pegasus. They climbed onto Moonbeam's back and launched skyward out of the clearing. The moon's rays struck the stones and the humming became a roar, as the beams activated the medicine wheel. White hot light flashed around the tops of the column, faster and faster, becoming a ring of lightning, blue forks sparking out of the circle.

The moon continued its climb and as it rose, the lightning sank lower down the column, striking runes which came alive, dancing with an inner life, as the stone changed from grey to a crystalized white. As each layer of rune activated, creatures of the forest entered the clearing, unicorns and fey folk and thunderbirds and sabretooth, every animal or being with a touch of magic in their blood. They were drawn like moths to a flame, unable to resist the pull of the moonlight.

Alfreda watched, open-mouthed, and tried to warn the creatures away, but they could not hear her, for her spiritual connection with them had been broken by the runes and the racing fever in her blood. She could not summon the bond. They were deaf to her call.

As the moonlight reached the bottom, the final course of runes flashed and light swept the circle, striking Caerwyn, Alfreda, Genii, and Artio. Lightning erupted in a bright white beam, which shot out from the circle and struck the moon with a thunderclap that flattened the trees on the edge of the clearing.

Caerwyn jerked as the full force of the moonbeam's bolt caught him full in the chest. His soul was torn from him and the agony was beyond his ability to comprehend. His mouth opened in a scream that was echoed by Alfreda's across the circle. They thrashed in their bonds, bodies shaking and jerking in the force of the lightning. Artio also shrieked and Genii lifted bodily into the air, jerking like a piñata struck by multiple sticks.

An earthquake rocked the ground and with the clap of a metal gong, the mountain above them exploded. The clearing shook, stones vibrating violently and suddenly a huge rent opened up directly below the white disk. The disk melted and oozed, flowing into the opening while ash and lava shot into the air.

From the middle of the blinding inferno, a figure of lava rose, its shape molded and formed by the cooling rock spewing from the flaming sinkhole. It rose, ever higher, until it climbed from the abyss on a swell of bubbling lava that carried it to the surface of the circle. As its feet cleared the lip, it took two steps onto solid ground. Two stories tall, the beast straightened, stretching its craggy body and lifted its massive head. A flat face with a wide forehead ended in a narrow snout with flaring nostrils. It snorted and flames shot from its nose. Long curling horns of flame curved away from either side of its head. A thick mat of fur covered its upper torso, and muscular arms ended in curled human fists. The legs of the beast ended in hoofs, and rippling across its skin was an ever-present flame. Its eyes were also flame, bright pools of lava that switched from orange to yellow to red, ever-changing.

The Daimon lifted its head and roared and then picked up a great scoop of lava and flung it into the stream of moonlight connecting the beam to the great orb of the moon, full on the horizon.

With a howl, the moon absorbed the steady flow of lava and from one moment to the next the pearly white surface bled, streaked with angry red colour. It swelled with the flow of lava and the moonlight changed to orange and the clearing burst into flame.

The touch of flame triggered the lid on the balance box, which sprang open with a click.

The box hummed and a cloud of blue mist rose into the air and encircled the Daimon, ice on fire. With a hiss at their touch, the Daimon flung lava at the mist, snarling when the mist parted, unharmed. Small fires ignited as the lava lurched through the air and fell to the ground.

With a roar, the Daimon twisted around frantic to escape the cooling touch of the spirits. Everywhere they touched the Daimon, his skin froze. The pain was so intense that it began to stamp around within the circle of stones, coming perilously close to trampling the unconscious occupants.

At that moment, Helga appeared at the head of the path screaming in fury. She flung out her hand and pointed it at the circle. As if thrown, the swirling shadows encircling her body launched themselves into the clearing. The Charun disturbed nothing as they swept between the monoliths, encircling the blue mists now shrouding the Daimon.

"Curse you, Caerwyn! How are you controlling the spirits yet? You cannot shield them from me, not any longer!" She stormed down to the edge of the stones, but she dared not enter the circle. The powers she had unleashed raged out of control, and Calleigh's potion provided only so much resistance. And there was something else...something more in the circle...a discordant resonance that hummed, disrupting the rebirth, both staccato and random at the same time.

The Daimon roared, swatting at the mists, ringing the circle with individual fires as it flung its muscular arms around and around. The Charun touched the antithesis of their being and the blue mists darkened as their souls were absorbed into the bottomless soul sucking void of darkness that is a Charun.

Mordecai, with his eyes squeezed shut, sat cross-legged on the cool grass on the opposite side of the valley from Helga. He clutched a smooth milky crystal in his hand. The crystal glowed bright blue, the light spilling out between his fingers. It flashed and trembled in his hands. Tears slid down his cheeks as he murmured to the crystal. He was hidden from Helga's eyes by the brush, but he sat perfectly still. His father lay flat and still by his side, his knuckles white with the tightness of his grip on his sword.

Mordecai's lips moved and the glow in his hand brightened to the intensity of a small sun until Hud worried that Helga would see light. Mordecai raised his head and as he gazed at the clearing, the blue mists of the spirits of the dead swirled brighter around the Daimon, spinning faster and faster, cooling its shell, freezing its hot blood. Slowly the Daimon darkened until with a final gasp, it began to shrink in size, collapsing inward smaller and smaller, drawn by the blue mists back to the balance box. With a snap, the lid sprang close. The beast vanished as though it had never existed.

Silence descended on the clearing.

* * *

A lone figure stirred on the ground. Genii woke, face down on the crystalized circle, rolling over and pushed up to a sitting position with one arm. The other arm was missing, and he blinked before the shock of the moment suspended, resolved into an agony of sensation. His arm was sitting a few feet from him on the ground. His scream echoed around the clearing as his body shook with reaction, the pain of severed nerves and sinews. His eyes slid away from the arm, staring around in disbelief. Artio's broken body sat at the edge of their circle, and he could see two other bodies by the stones, slumped over and still. He crawled across the space to Artio's side and pulled her bloody body to his with his remaining arm then collapsed down beside her, stroking her hair with his remaining hand. Genii howled, but this pain was of the heart. He wanted nothing more than to join her in death. He would die with her in his arms.

A foot appeared by his head and he looked up, eyes straining to focus. A shimmering form stood before him. *I am dying* he thought and somehow couldn't muster the strength to care. His eyes closed and his breathing slowed.

* * *

Helga's face twisted with anger. She bent down and placed her hands on Genii's head, and he howled with pain, back arching. A blue mist rose from his body which Helga ignored. When her hands lifted, he stared at her, glassy-eyed. His arm had been reattached (he did not know when). At Helga's silent command, he lifted Artio's broken body into his arms and silently followed his new mistress out of the clearing.

Helga did not even glance at the corpses of her brother and other sister. As she stepped from the clearing, their bodies crumbled and turned to dust. They were no more.

Epilogue

MORDECAI BEN-MOSES was a brilliant wizard. Raised in the rich kingdom of Cathair and housed in the royal household, he had the best of everything. Fine robes and fine chambers, and an endless supply of books to study and entertain him were mere bonuses to his true purpose in life.

Mordecai Ben-Moses was also reclusive. He was happy to spend his time studying, honing his skills and preparing for the future. He was eldest of the royal children, but as the son of the king before he was made king, he was ineligible to take the throne. Not that he had an interest in doing so.

As a half-brother he downplayed his semi-royal heritage.

It was also centuries ago. No one remembered those days. He was the last of that line, blessed with long life due to the magic running through his veins. Instead, he took on the role of counsellor, and prepared the later princes and kings in their duties as the royal Spirit Shields of Cathair, teaching them the sanctity of their role and its gravity.

It did not bother Mordecai, for he had known his duty since the age of seven. Teaching the princes kept him close to the castle, permitting him free access to the most sensitive of areas. He was able to wander the castle grounds and the hidden passages below, monitoring the sacred trust placed in him by Caerwyn and Alfreda.

Only he knew where their souls resided. His time would come. The spirits demanded it. The fate of the world hung in the balance. He would be called on, before the end of his days, to restore the true king.

He placed his hand on the balance box, and it murmured to him...as always.

Did you enjoy *Soul Survivor*?
Don't let the journey end!
Check out this free excerpt from
Seer of Souls, Book One of the
Spirit Shield Saga

PROLOGUE

THE BABY GAVE a feeble, barely discernable kick. Its twin had ceased movement but not with the natural stillness of slumber. Poison moved through their premature bodies, oozing along their tiny veins, a burning acid in their blood.

Mordecai lifted his hand from the woman's sweaty forehead. Gwen's panicked eyes locked onto his sad grey ones. She clutched her distended belly as another wave of pain ripped through her.

"It must be poison! This is more than simple birthing pangs." She coughed and the motion made bile rise in her throat. Gwen clutched at Mordecai's left hand, gripping it so tight the knuckles of her hand whitened. "It's reaching the babies! Mordecai, what do we do?"

Straightening his lanky frame, he released her hand and wandered over to the tall mullioned window of the bartizan room. His sweeping brows pinched together in a frown as he gazed unseeingly at the silent courtyard below him. Purple wisteria climbed the ashlar walls of the castle, revealing their stark outlines. A fresh breeze stirred the heavy tapestry curtains as lightning flashed, highlighting the roiling clouds, puffing in eager anticipation of the storm breaking over the castle.

Her seclusion was for her protection. Gwen's grief over Prince Alexander's failure to return from his most recent patrol with the Kingsmen twisted in her gut, accentuating the pain of the poison. The prince and all of the Kingsmen in his unit had been slaughtered by Primordials in a sudden vicious attack. This sorrowful news had arrived on the heels of the king's death from a heart attack a week prior. The kingdom was reeling from the double disaster. *And now it's my turn. I am the target*, she thought.

Gwen coughed and froth formed in her mouth, drowning her thoughts. Her lungs attempted to fill but failed. Intense pressure gripped her chest as though a large man with a booted foot stood on it compressing it. She pushed aside her discomfort and staggered over to join the wizard at the window. She clutched a handful of his grey robe sleeve, partly to gain his attention and partly to keep from sinking to the floor.

"Please, Mordecai, I must save my babies! What can I do? There has to be a way to help them. Between your magic and my heritage, there *must* be a way."

Mordecai's mouth drooped beneath his long white beard. "I can only think of one solution, Gwen" he said gently. "You must pass the mother bond to me." Tears sparked in her almond-shaped eyes as he locked his to hers. "I think we both know that you cannot survive this poison." He squeezed her hands. "We need to convince Alcina the babes have died with you."

Gwen's liquid green eyes searched and found steely resolve reflected in his grey ones. She nodded once and unconsciously rubbed one hand across her protruding belly, where the foot of the lone stirring child pushed against the thin protection of her skin.

"We need do this quickly, Gwen. The birth will take most of your remaining strength, and they must be born alive in order to pass the bond."

She groaned again as a hard contraction took her. The twisting pain of a poison-filled cramp left her gasping for air as she sank to her knees beside the wizard. She raised her head, panting. "I do not think that is a problem, Mordecai."

Mordecai gently eased her onto her back, on the cold stone floor. Reaching inside his pocket, he took out a clear crystal stone and placed it between her cold hands, clasping them with in his own. Together, they began to chant.

* * *

The late-day sun streamed through the garden-view windows of the bartizan room. Dust motes stirred in a breeze heavy with the smell of damp earth and wisteria. A few trailing clouds scuttled across the sky in an attempt to catch the storm moving off to the east, low rumbles fading softly into the distance.

With a groan, Mordecai sank back to his knees on the polished floor beside the princess. Gwen's sweat-soaked brown hair curled damply over her curiously shaped ears. Dark circles shadowed her eyes; eyes that stared back at him from a deathly pale face.

She lay on the floor, her bloodstained gown bunched to one side. Beside her, wrapped in cotton swaddling, were two newborn infants, a boy and a girl.

Both children were dead.

A tiny red birthmark, resembling the shape of an oak leaf, adorned the right side of each smooth cheek. The tattoos faded away before his eyes. Mordecai smiled a grim smile and trailed a thin finger down the soft cheeks where the tattoos had appeared so briefly, sensing the residue of magic under the skin.

Gwen lifted her hand and caressed the cheeks of her two babes. A hot tear trickled out of the corner of her eye. She would never know them, nor they her.

Mordecai lifted the children and placed them in her arms. She hugged them and wept silently, tears streaming down onto the cherubic face of the closest child.

Gwen's mournful eyes lifted to the man standing beside her.

"Are they truly safe now, Mordecai?" Her weak voice shook with supressed emotion.

"They are as safe as we can make them, Gwen."

She touched his sleeve. "Thank you," she murmured weakly. "You have been a true friend." She stiffened, sucking in a hard breath that ended abruptly. Her eyes widened as the soul in their emerald depths faded away. Her hand slipped from his sleeve and thudded to the floor.

Mordecai gently closed her eyes, squeezing his own shut to dam the tears sliding down his whiskered face.

"Sleep well, Gwen, and welcome the peaceful embrace of the Mother."

He staggered to a chair by the open window. Leaning out over the stone ledge, he saw a dead eagle on the stones below. He dropped back into the chair beside the window and gazed out at the setting sun. The last of the storm clouds faded into the distance. Little did they know that they carried the hopes and dreams of the world in their midst.

Pain stabbed into Mordecai's chest and he sucked in a deep breath. If his calculations were correct, he had little more than a half hour left. The poison was completing its job.

Well, his task was finished. What would be would be. Eyes opened wide, he watched the sun creep toward the horizon. The rays of the setting sun blazed through the retreating clouds, glowing pink and orange. His lips curved with satisfaction. It was done.

* * *

The tall, regal woman burst into the room, cruel eyes sweeping the creeping shadows. Her contingent of guards with lanterns held aloft quickly encircled her and then spread out along the sides of the room.

She gazed around at the scene before her. "Search the room for others. Check to see that no one is alive," she snapped at the guards.

She marched up to the woman lying on the floor cuddling her two babes. Frowning, she stepped around the bodies and moved over to the man in the chair.

He sat staring glassy-eyed out the window. She felt for a pulse in his neck and located a faint pulse under the curve of his chin.

"The wizard still lives!" she screamed. "Find the mage. Hurry!"

She snapped her fingers, calling the two guards standing closest. "Pick him up, and move him to the lower dungeon. Secure him with two guards on the door at all times. His head is to be shaven before he awakes and it must remain shaven or his powers will return."

She grabbed Mordecai's whiskered jaw in her long-nailed hand and shook his slack face. "Poor bald wizard," she murmured to him. "You hoped to be dead before I arrived, didn't you? Soon, you will tell me all your secrets, starting with this room. I will know the truth of this before you die." She released his face. "Take him away!"

Whirling around, she barked to the other guards crowding the room. "Burn the bodies—immediately! There will be no Remembrance Eulogy for them. They are unworthy of the honour. It is reserved for true royalty"—she nudged Gwen's body with her toe—"and she is not royalty! Filthy heathen!"

Furious, she stormed from the room, her black silk skirts snapping in her wake.

* * *

Soul Survivor is the prequel to *Seer of Souls,* book one of the Spirit Shield Saga and a 2016 FINALIST for the DANTE ROSSETTI Awards for Young Adult Fiction!

Author Susan Faw

Professional by day, book nerd and fantasy champion by night, Susan is a masked crusader for the fantastical world. Championing mythical rights, she quells uprisings and battles infidels who would slay the lifeblood of her pen. It's all in a night's work, for this whirlwind writer. Welcome to the quest.

You can visit her online at:

http://susanfaw.com

Follow Susan Faw on:

https://www.facebook.com/SusanFaw

https://twitter.com/susandfaw

https://www.pinterest.com/susandfaw

CPSIA information can be obtained
at www.ICGtesting.com
Printed in the USA
FSOW02n0729050118
43089FS